Ac|

Thanks to my sister and editor, Jeune Brown, and pre-publication readers Alecia Kraus, Derf and Mary Ann Maitland, and Sally Mehring for their patience with me, and for making this a better book. Thanks to my daughter, Angela Suehr for the rose photo, and my niece and graphic artist, Tracie Stambaugh for the Lost Soul cover design. Thanks also to Doug Becker, Derf Maitland, Robert Michels, Jeff Rebert, and Father Lawrence Sherdel for their encouragement and support with this book.

Disclaimer

This book is a work of fiction. Any references to real people, events, establishments, organizations, or locales are intended solely to provide a sense of authenticity and are used fictitiously. All other characters, incidents, and dialogues are drawn from the author's imagination and are not to be construed as real.

Mary,
forever.

Table of Contents

Lost Soul of the Black Rose: A Vampire's Confession
A Novella by Gardy Lawrence

PROLOGUE

We always believed that we were Irish. Were not most of the

local Lawrence families descended from immigrants from

somewhere in the United Kingdom? Did not most of the local

Lawrence families have some ancestral connection to the small

village of Irishtown, in rural Adams County, Pennsylvania? Were

they not all devout Irish Catholics tied to the parish at Conewago

Chapel or at Annunciation B.V.M. in McSherrystown, or one of the

other neighboring Catholic communities?

That was my world. It was a world driven by Catholicism. It

made sense to me. My father, and his father before him, had

believed in the Irish Catholic origin for our bloodline. I remember

vividly my father's anger when I remarked to my soon-to-be brother-

in-law that the votive candles burning in the front of the church were merely a money maker for the Annunciation parish. We are

Catholic, and that is unconditional.

This belief took an interesting turn when a cousin in the Colgan

family (the matriarch of that family being a Lawrence) presented me

with a brief history of the Colgans, and I discovered through their

research that we were not really Lawrence descendants at all.

We were German and descended from the immigrant Moritz

Lorentz, who arrived with his family in Philadelphia in 1732.

Through the efforts of Marian Bale and Diane Lawrence

Krumrine, much has been researched and documented regarding

Moritz and his descendants in the <u>Lawrence Legacy</u>, published in

1999. The one aspect that has remained consistent is this

Pennsylvania German family's devotion when it comes to their faith

in the teachings of the Roman Catholic Church.

It was during my continued genealogical research into the

Lorentz family and our other ancestral lines in the Pennsylvania

Room of the Hanover Public Library that this story began to unfold.

Who was this Percival Lorentz? Where does he fit, or not fit, into the large line of Moritz Lorentz's 13,000 or so descendants? There are no definite records, only an obscure article to be found here and there: an unmarked grave, a temporarily missing teenage girl, an irate father, witchcraft in York County, possible animal attacks, stolen blood, and a mansion destroyed by fire.

Where does this all lead? What does this all mean? Was there a "black sheep" in the Lorentz line that other descendants would rather see forgotten?

Who is this Percival Lorentz? Records only indicate a birth year, 1912 - , with parents Jeremiah and Genevieve, and siblings Sofia, Alexa, and Sarah. Where to and why did this Lorentz family disappear? What has become of Percival Lorentz? How long has he lived beyond the dash behind his year of birth?

The question remains. Here is the story of young Percival Lorentz as I was best able to develop it through the piecing together of information from the aforementioned obscure articles.

While delivering flowers for Cremer Florist in the early 1970's, I would have arrangements for Mrs. J. W. Gitt, who resided in the large mansion on the south slope of the Pigeon Hills just off of Broadway extended. I often thought, as I made my way up the winding lane to the Gitt mansion, that it resembled Collinwood from the afternoon television soap opera, Dark Shadows. Little did I know what had occurred in a similar home located just one quarter of a mile to the east.

THE SETTING

Hanover, Pennsylvania. Not Bon Temps, Louisiana, or Collinsport, Maine, or Forks, Washington, or Mystic Falls, Virginia, but Hanover, Pennsylvania. Yes, Hanover, a sleepy, small rural town known for shoes, potato chips, water wheels, and nearby horse farms, lying in Pennsylvania's rolling hills just north of the Mason-Dixon Line. Founded in 1763 and named for Hannover, Germany, it seems these towns have much more in common than merely a name.

Located just north of Hanover are the Pigeon Hills, and on the south slope above the town rise the silhouettes of two majestic English style mansions. Approximately one quarter of a mile to the east of the well-known Gitt mansion stands the Lorentz house on Hershey Hill. Locals liked to joke in the 1920's that Youngs Road should have been know as Editor's Alley, with the neighbors J.W. Gitt and Jeremiah Lorentz living there, as they are the editors of

York's Gazette and Daily and the Hanover Record-Herald,

respectively. The name does fit. While the Gitt Mansion was built

for the Gitt family in 1927, the Lorentz's purchased their home,

designed and built by the same contractor, using a similar English

style, in 1928. From the valley below, the huge gap in the tree line

where the Lorentz home stood is clearly evident, even today. The

only remaining trace of what these immense homes looked like back

then is the Gitt mansion today. Even in all of its splendor, the house

remains merely a shadow of its former self, with nearly half of the

original mansion torn down after Gitt's mother-in-law passed away

in 1935.

It is in this pristine setting that sixteen year old Percival Lorentz

learns of his infliction, and is sent reeling emotionally and physically

as the intended cure becomes a curse for all eternity. His father's

determination to reverse the premature aging disease is successful,

but little does Jeremiah Lorentz know that the price is his son's soul,

and that Percival has become immortal.

The terror that is unleashed in the Pigeon Hills and the Hanover area leads to a panic that eventually lands on the Lorentz's doorstep. This fear causes the eventual destruction of the Lorentz home by fire in late 1930. Was it torched by an angry mob attempting to eliminate the source of the rumored vampire attacks in the area? Or was it burned out of spite by a young and jealous scorned lover? Fortunately for the Lorentz's, the last issue of the Hanover Record-Herald ran on November 4, 1930, and the family was in the process of relocating.

On the fateful evening of the fire, only Percival Lorentz and his friend, Maria, were near the house. They were warned, and escaped up the slope of the Pigeon Hills, where they sat, embraced, and wept as the great house was burned to the ground.

And so, the setting for this novella, <u>Lost Soul of the Black Rose: A Vampire's Confession</u>, is established. This is the first of a trilogy about the life of a young vampire in Hanover.

THE DISEASE

"The last enemy to be destroyed is death."
1 Corinthians 15:26

"O death where is thy sting? O grave where is thy victory?"
1 Corinthians 15:55

Gettysburg Times, Thursday, June 5, 1930
Investigate "Grave" In Pigeon Hills
Ghosts Active, Country Folk Tell York County Authorities

Spooks are again abroad in the Pigeon Hills and reports of spells and incantations make the residents of that section of York County shudder with dread and consternation.

The attention of District Attorney Ralph Fisher of York, has been called by Frank Hoke, Menges Mills, to the finding of what appears to be a new-made grave in the woods near the home of Bert Hoover, residing near Gnatstown, about two miles north of Menges Mills.

Hoover is reported to have found the "grave" close to his farm. On a tree nearby is carved the word "Beware" with the rude depiction of a skull and crossbones. The grave was found several days ago and reported to District Attorney Fisher Tuesday. Mr. Fisher has promised an investigation.

Jeremiah and Genevieve Lorentz sat stunned in the drawing room

of their house on Hershey Hill. Dr. John Meisenhelter had just

arrived from his office on Broadway in Hanover and given them the

11

devastating news about the blood test results that he had received

from the lab in nearby York. How could this be? Their seemingly

healthy 16 year old son son, Percival, destined to the fate of an early

grave because medicine has no cure for the disease which has

afflicted him. The doctor simply said it is Progeria, a rare congenital

abnormality characterized by premature and rapid aging, with the

affected individual appearing in childhood as an aged person and

having a shortened life span.

Genevieve was nearly hysterical; her first-born child inflicted by

such a malady. Why? Aging is a natural process of the life cycle:

birth, aging, and then death. That is how it usually goes. We age

naturally, and as we become older, our bodies are growing older, and

in turn, our bodies make changes to adjust to its changing self.

However, one disease threatens this natural process, and that disease

is Progeria.

The doctor went on to explain that there are two types of

Progeria. One is called Hutchinson-Gilford Progeria Syndrome, or HGPS. A child born with HGPS has transparent skin as an infant, and a small, fragile body, like that of an elderly person. Most children, and most patients with HGPS have an average life-span of 13 years, with a range of 8 to 21 years.

The doctor informed them that Percival has the other form of the disease, called the Werner Syndrome, which is also known as Adult Progeria. It is named after Otto Werner, a German medical student, who first identified the disease in 1904. This form of Progeria is a recessive gene, which means that two recessive genes of this disease are needed to manifest the illness; therefore, two parents carrying Werner Syndrome genes have the possibility of passing it on to their children. Adult Progeria affects patients approaching or in their early to middle teenage years, usually during the time puberty is due. Werner Syndrome patients develop normally until puberty. No other signs are shown until patients reach their thirties, which is when many age-affected disorders begin coming into light. Such diseases as cataracts, diabetes, severe hardening of the arteries and cancer may appear.

Jeremiah Lorentz persistently asked what can be done, and the doctor's response remained steadfast, "There is no cure for Werner Syndrome." Dr. Meisenhelter could offer no remedies, only sympathy for the family as they attempted to process this dreadful news. What a devastating cloud has been cast over this happy and healthy family!

Life is peaceful in the Pigeon Hills just north of Hanover, where Jeremiah is the owner and editor of the Hanover Record-Herald. How will Jeremiah and Genevieve break this horrible news to Percival and his three younger sisters, Sofia, Alexa, and little Sarah, who love their older brother so much? It is almost certain that life in the great house on Hershey Hill will never be the same.

Percival and his sisters handled the news in a fashion that is consistent with the way teens show no real sense of urgency about their own mortality. His response was a casual, "Well, thirty-something is a long way off, and I'm not going to let this "syndrome thing" bother me now." He then went off like he did on so many

other spring days and walked the freshly tilled fields in the flatlands

to the south of the great house, along Gitt Run, in search of new

Indian relics and arrowheads to enhance his growing collection.

Percival possesses a keen interest in the early inhabitants of the

land that they were forced to share with the European settlers who

had headed West of the Susquehanna River. While he is named for

one of the fabled Knights of the Round Table, he views himself as

more of a kindred spirit with the Native Americans, as was his hero,

James Fenimore Cooper's, Hawkeye. As he handles each relic, he

can feel a closeness, or sense of spiritual connection, with the last

human hand that had warmed the blackish-gray rhyolite stone that

had been so intricately shaped. For a young man his age, Percival

has become a skilled surface hunter and, as he locates a relic, he

observes it on the ground and reflects respectfully about the Native

American who last touched the stone artifact. Each find is definitely

more to him than just an object to be collected and tossed into an old

15

cigar box.

His father, on the other hand, remained devastated by the news of the affliction that would haunt this household for years to come. Jeremiah felt that there had to be something that could be done to reverse the progression of this dreadful disease in his son. Of course, he and Genevieve pursued the usual course of prayer that would be expected from a devout Pennsylvania German Catholic family. The entire family prayed together and begged the Almighty for intercession. Surely they had done nothing to warrant this type of circumstance to be leveled against one of their loved ones.

The Lorentz family was one of those German immigrant families that had arrived in Philadelphia in the 1730's and settled near Caspar Wistar's Glass Works in Salem County, New Jersey. They endured harassment from the troops of England's King George II for practicing their Catholic faith. Eventually they fled to Berks County, Pennsylvania, and the Jesuit mission at Goshenhoppen, located near present day Bally. It was from there that some members of the family migrated to the Conewago Valley and the Hanover Area.

How could a God that they serve so nobly turn on them and allow

this to happen to Percival?

For Jeremiah, it was becoming more and more difficult to trust

the conventional medicine of the early twentieth century, as well as

the healing powers of a God that he was sure had forsaken him.

Everyone who knew Jeremiah saw the sullen look on his face

becoming deeper every day. Family and friends began to keep their

distance for fear that they would touch off one of his rages against

medicine and his Creator. Jeremiah was desperate. As the head of

this household, he had to come up with a solution to his son's

predicament. He felt the weight of the world on his shoulders as he

looked into the innocent eyes of his young children and their mother,

who so faithfully depended on him for some sort of plan.

Then one early December evening in 1929, while working at the

Record-Herald, he reviewed a reporter's story about the recent

anniversary of a murder that had taken place in southern York

County involving a spell from a book of healings and remedies

called <u>The Long Lost Friend</u>. He thought for a moment, and then

put the article aside and moved on to something else. Work was

difficult these days as Jeremiah could not get the thought of

Percival's possible premature death out of his mind. He was

obsessed.

One night, a few days after first seeing the story about the murder

in southern York County, Jeremiah again read the summary which

he had folded up and placed in his vest pocket. The story read as

follows:

The Murder of Nelson Rehmeyer

John H. Blymire, a pow-wow doctor, or Pennsylvania Dutch witch,
had, for years, been suffering from illness and bad luck. When
another pow-wow doctor, Nellie Noll, also known as the River
Witch of Marietta, told him he had come under the hex of witch
doctor Nelson D. Rehmeyer, Blymire decided to retaliate by
breaking into Rehmeyer's home in search of a book of spells. Noll
also informed Blymire that burning the book or burying a lock of
Rehmeyer's hair would remove the Hex. Upon arrival to his farm
house in North Hopewell Township, they encountered Rehmeyer
himself.

Blymire and his two young accomplices, John Curry and Wilbert Hess, murdered, mutilated, and then burned Rehmeyer's body. The murder took place exactly one minute past midnight on November 28, 1928. They were unsuccessful in locating his copy of <u>The Long Lost Friend</u>; however, Blymire felt the hex lifted when Rehmeyer died. In the trial that followed, the country was shocked to learn of the existence of 20th century witchcraft, especially in quiet York County, Pennsylvania.

It was after reading this story for the second time that Jeremiah Lorentz decides two things: he will obtain a copy of <u>The Long Lost Friend</u>, and he will contact a Pennsylvania-German faith healer; either Professor Resh, on Carlisle Street in Hanover, or Nellie Noll, the River Witch of Marietta.

He was desperate. What did he have to lose? Although he had also discovered that the York County Medical Society was planning legal action against practitioners who were believed to be witches, Jeremiah Lorentz knew what he had to do.

THE CURE

"Do not turn to mediums or wizards; do not seek them out, to be defiled by them: I am the Lord your God." Leviticus 19:31

"A badly scared man or a doomed man will turn to anyone who gives him hope."
Cornelius Weygant, Pennsylvania Dutch writer, on powwowing

For Nellie Noll, the River Witch of Marietta, the past year has been particularly troubling. Prior to 1928, she had declared that she would no longer be taking any new patients seeking her powwowing expertise. After curing patients in Marietta for four generations, Nellie Noll was finished.

Then in the late summer and autumn of that same year, out of compassion or arguably financial need, she agreed to consult with fellow witch, John Blymire. After several meetings, she identified Nelson Rehmeyer, the witch of Rehmeyer's Hollow in southern

20

York County, as the hexmeister or braucher who had put the spell on him. In a subsequent meeting, she indicated that Rehmeyer had also been responsible for the hex on the Milton J. Hesses, as well as John Curry.

She instructed them to get a lock of Rehmeyer's hair and the copy of his witch's bible, The Long LostFriend. They were then to burn the book and bury the hair six to eight feet underground. According to the River Witch of Marietta, after completing this task, the spell or curse would be lifted. Blymire and his two accomplices attempted to carry out her instructions and, in the process, murdered Nelson Rehmeyer.

Had the cloud of the Rehmeyer murder case not been cast over her Front Street, Marietta home, Nellie Noll would probably never have agreed to meet with Jeremiah Lorentz to discuss the possibility of healing his son, Percival, in early January of 1930.On the other hand, had the Lorentz's not had such a strong foundation in the Catholic Faith, they would never have sought out such a cure.

Because many of the Pennsylvania German healings find the sources of their incantations in the Bible, like many of the Pennsylvania German Catholics, the Lorentz's believed that this spiritual healing may hold the answers to reversing Percival's fate, as the practiced medicine of the 1920's could not.

To further support their desperate rationale, they also found comfort in the fact that the author of The Long Lost Friend, John George Hohman, was a devout Catholic himself, from the Reading area in Berks County, Pennsylvania. Hohman states with no reservation: "Whoever carries this book with him is safe from all his enemies, visible or invisible; and whoever has this book with him cannot die without the holy corpse of Jesus Christ, nor drown in any water, nor burn up in any fire, nor can any unjust sentence be passed upon him. So help me."

The River Witch of Marietta, Nellie Noll, listened carefully as Jeremiah Lorentz detailed the diagnosis and prognosis for his son's future. Percival did not make a sound as he watched in disbelief while the old woman examined him with her piercing blue eyes. He

felt as though she was peering into the very depths of his soul. The

youthfulness in those blue eyes was in sharp contrast with the

ninety-plus year old features the white haired witch otherwise

possessed. The River Witch of Marietta never said a word as she

studied Percival for what seemed like an eternity. Suddenly she

closed her eyes and murmured, "I believe I can do this."

She then opened her eyes and stared deeply into Percival's eyes

and stated, "My belief is not sufficient in and of itself. You, young

man, must also possess faith in my abilities."

A common practice among witches was the use of dove's blood,

taken internally, several drops at a time, twice daily. This elixir was

expected to bring lasting results. But in this case, the River Witch

felt that she needed more cleansing than the dove's blood would

provide. Dove's blood works for the relief of the most difficult

cases, but more was needed to lead to a cure for Percival. It would

take the transfusion of human blood in conjunction with Hohman's special incantation to heal Percival. She chanted, "Christ's cross and Christ's crown, Christ Jesus's colored blood, be thou every hour good."

Nellie Noll then instructed Jeremiah to hire a private duty nurse and to have her remove two units of blood from Percival's left arm and immediately replace those two units with two units of blood of a matching type, taken from immediate family members who are known not to carry the disease. This process should be carried out monthly over the next three months. Jeremiah indicated that Percival's teenage sisters, Sofia and Alexa, would serve as the donors.

The River Witch also indicated that Percival must repeat the following incantation every day for two weeks after receiving his sisters' blood: "God, the Father, is before me; God, the Son, is beside me; God, the Holy Ghost, is behind me. Whoever now is stronger than these three persons may come, by day or night, to attack me."

24

Jeremiah, the careful newspaper man that he was, copied the witch's instructions word-for-word. Percival had listened intently, although he was not sure how much faith he really had in the River Witch, he possessed an unconditional trust in his father and indicated his willingness to comply with all of her instructions.

Jeremiah and Percival departed from Marietta and headed west across the Susquehanna River and into York County. Percival felt fatigued and slept. Jeremiah reflected on the day's events and finally felt as though he had some inner peace. Could it be that her healing spell was already at work? Jeremiah couldn't wait to put the new treatment plan into action with the rest of the family, who were anxiously awaiting their return to the house on Hershey Hill.

THE DONORS

"The Lord is faithful; he will strengthen you and guard you from the
evil one."
2 Thessalonians 3:3

Percival believes that he is beginning to feel the effects of the

incantations and the blood replacement treatments recommended by

Nellie Noll, the River Witch of Marietta. According to her

instructions, Percival's blood is let from his left arm and he is

immediately given units of blood to replace it intravenously in his

right arm. Venesection, more commonly known as "bleeding", was

a medical practice that had survived since the Middle Ages.

Percival was not overly enthused about this facet of his treatment.

He remembers reading somewhere that one of his heroes, Robin

Hood, had in fact died as a result of this practice. He looked into his father's eyes and saw Jeremiah's determined look and nodded his

head in agreement.

The new blood had to be from donors of the same blood type and

fortunately for Percival, his two oldest sisters, Sofia and Alexa, were

perfect matches. With the love and affection they feel for their older

brother, they are more than willing to do whatever it takes to reverse

the terrible prognosis that Percival has been given.

During the second of these blood transfusions, Percival begins to

feel extremely weak and nauseous as he lies there after letting blood

and beginning the process of receiving a unit of Sofia's replacement

blood. He does not remember becoming weak and blacking out.

When he awakens, he seems to lose all control as he watches her

blood flow from its container, through the transparent tube, and into

his body. He quickly sits up, removes the tube from the IV port in

his right arm, and begins to drink the blood directly from the tube.

The satisfaction that he receives is of a level that he never could

have imagined. It is a complete state of euphoria such as he has never experienced.

He hears footsteps in the hall. Monica Myers, the private duty nurse the family has hired is returning to his room. Percival quickly reinserts the tube and lies there quietly as though nothing has happened.

"How are you feeling?" asks the nurse.

Percival replies, "Well, to tell you the truth, I've never felt better." The flavor of Sofia's blood will cause him to place a fixation on his sister that will be his nemesis in the days to come.

One of those cool early spring evenings is being experienced in the Pigeon Hills. Sofia, in her nightgown, stretches across her bed reading and enjoying the evening breeze. The house on Hershey Hill has been extremely peaceful lately as Percival appears to be making strides with his treatments and there is a feeling of relief within the Lorentz household.

Suddenly, Sofia's bedroom door is thrust open and into the room bursts Percival, with a wild expression on his face. His eyes glare and his lips tremble. He is drooling and his mouth is partially open. He stares at his startled sister and slowly begins to approach her. She recoils in fear and backs away on her bed.

Just as he reaches the side of the bed, there is a loud rustling in the window and a large dove-like bird has landed there and is staring directly into Percival's eyes. The noisy arrival of the bird startles him, and he suddenly relaxes and just gazes at Sofia and says, "My dear sister Sofia, I am very sorry that I entered so abruptly and frightened you so. Please forgive me."

They both glance in the direction of the open window, and the dove-like bird is gone. It is obvious to Sofia that Percival really has no idea as to the extent of the fit of rage that he had exhibited. He quickly turns and leaves her room as abruptly as he had entered it.

Sofia slept lightly that night and said nothing to anyone about her encounter with her brother earlier that evening. Unknown to Sofia, her younger sister, Alexa, had experienced a similar incident with their beloved brother.

By far, the closest sibling that Percival has to a brother is his middle sister, Alexa. At fourteen years of age, she is still very much interested in what her older brother is doing when he goes off on his excursions into the fields and woods. For many years he allowed her to accompany him but, lately, things have changed.

Since his meeting with the woman in Marietta and the start of the transfusions, Percival seems to be growing more and more distant. When Alexa seeks his attention or wants to spend time with him, he makes excuses and goes off on his own.

Late one early spring afternoon, Alexa is passing the time searching for chipmunks in and around the large woodpile that is stacked to the rear of the great house. She becomes excited when she locates one very near to her. As she reaches for an axe to move it out of her way, she accidentally cuts the palm of her hand on the exposed blade.

Alexa remains calm, and seeing Percival strolling down the lane as he returns from one of his walks, she runs toward him shouting,

"I've cut my hand!"

Percival abruptly responds, "Well, go inside and see Mother. What do you want me to do?"

Alexa insists, "No, you must help me now!"

She shoves her cut and bleeding palm right in front of his face. Upon seeing the fresh blood oozing across the pale palm of her hand, Percival grabs her wrist and starts to frantically suck the blood from her wound.

Alexa shouts, "Stop it!"

She attempts to pull her hand away but she cannot. Percival is much too strong for her to break his grip on her slender wrist. Overcome with fright, she continues the struggle to pull her palm from Percival's mouth.

Suddenly, the dove-like bird lands in their midst and violently flutters its wings about their feet. Percival is startled and lets go of Alexa's wrist. His face is a dreadful sight with Alexa's blood smeared all around his mouth. Alexa turns to run, but stops and

31

looks back at Percival standing there beside the dove-like bird.

As their eyes meet, Percival shouts, "I'm sorry. I just wanted to stop the bleeding."

Alexa presses on the wound with her other hand and stares at her brother in disbelief. As the bird flies away, Alexa says, "I'm going inside to get this cleaned up right now." With that, she turns and runs off toward the house, leaving Percival standing alone in the lane.

THE HOPE

"What can be seen is temporary, but what cannot be seen is eternal."
2 Corinthians 4:18

As Percival follows the flight of this persistent dove-like bird into the trees on the southern slope of the Pigeon Hills, he is led to a small cove where several fresh springs run forth and produce the stream along which the Native Americans must have lived and hunted. At first, Percival sees the bird land on a small rock outcropping, and he looks away for a moment. When he looks back he is astonished to see a pale figure of a teenage girl in what appears to be Native American garb seated there watching him. As it is near evening, his vision is very acute so he knows immediately that this is no dream. The two watch one another for a few moments…for what seems like an eternity, and the girl speaks first.

33

"My attention was drawn to you as I watched you searching for the artifacts left by my people when they inhabited this area. I knew that you were different when I witnessed the reverence with which you treasured even the smallest of relics that connected you with our past."

Percival is stunned. The girl continues.

"I also know that you are troubled, and that you are trying to control the changes that have taken place within you recently. I, too, had to adjust to major changes at your age, when I was taken by the French and Shawnee from my English family and adopted by the Senecas. I did not understand everything that was happening to me, but I still retained my sense of what was right and what was wrong. I tried to treat my captors with respect and when they saw this behavior, they reacted to it favorably. I knew that I could not change what had happened to me, but I could help to establish the path for my future, even though it would be far different than I could ever have imagined."

Percival listens intently as she continues.

"I want very much to help you. You know that the feeling of desire that you have for human blood is wrong. The lust that you have for the blood of your sisters is wrong."

Percival begins to weep.

"With the respect that you have shown for our culture, I can help you to learn our ways of silently hunting small game so as not to be detected. You will learn to feed on the blood of your animal prey rather than the blood of the innocent human victims that you are now craving."

She pauses for a few moments and then says, "Please hear my words. We will meet again and discuss this possibility for your future. When the cravings start, think about me. Look for the pigeon, and I will be near you. Good bye."

As the girl turns and starts fading into the evening mist, Percival shouts, "Wait!"

She stops and looks back over her shoulder. Percival again

shouts, "What shall I call you?"

She smiles and answers, "Martha."

Percival stands there and watches as she fades away. For the first time in a long while, he feels a faint glimmer of hope.

As Percival begins to spend more and more time roaming the slopes and ridges of the Pigeon Hills, he can feel the changes taking place within his mind and body. His thirst for raw blood has become insatiable. He definitely needs the help that was promised by his new confidant, Martha. He is working hard to overcome the desires that would build up for the consumption of his sisters' blood. He knows that he will only have access to their blood one more time during the scheduled transfusion; and then only if the nurse leaves the room for a period of time. He is becoming frightened and desperate.

On one of his woods roaming endeavors in the spring, he ventures to the western extreme of the Pigeon Hills, which takes him across the Abbottstown Pike and into Oxford Township in Adams

36

County. It is on this trek that he discovers one of his favorite secluded locations. Here he can reflect on what he has become and identify the disciplines needed to live with his condition. Thanks to his meeting with Martha, he refuses to call it a curse.

This site is the ruins of an old Trappist Monastery which had been abandoned when the Monks migrated further southwest into Kentucky in the early 1800's. It is a quiet and tranquil place, and he feels at peace here surrounded by the varieties of phlox that have overgrown the old monastic gardens. He discovers that the ruins of the old well still contain water that is cool and refreshing. He will have future rendezvous with Martha at this site, but his second such meeting occurs at the place known as High Rock.

Percival's emotions run high and low, and they are heightened to the extreme by the transition to vampirism that he is going through. On a day that he is feeling particularly depressed, he has made his way to High Rock and is thinking that if he is still human enough, he can throw himself off the rocks and end it all here. He has given this

37

much thought and feels that he can no longer live with the monster that he is becoming.

Approaching the rocky ledge, Percival turns to the sound of the pigeon as it lands behind him. Martha takes him by the hand and leads him away from the ledge to a shaded area where they sit together upon a rock. Percival, in a state of disbelief, gazes into Martha's eyes and begins to sob.

"You're real." he remarks. "I could feel the touch of your hand."

"I am real to you." replies Martha.

He rubs his teary eyes in disbelief and says, "I thought you were just a vision or an apparition of some sort." Percival rambles on about hearing that many recipients of Pennsylvania Dutch healing spells such as his, have had experiences with what they described as Indian guides.

Martha responds, "I am much more than that for you. We want very much to help you through this plight."

"Wait, who is we?" asks Percival.

Martha then informs Percival that she does not possess all of the knowledge or skills necessary to teach him everything that he needs to know about acquiring animal sources for the blood that will sustain him. She then points into a small grove of mountain laurel to the figure of a white teenage boy dressed like one of the woodsmen that you would find described in Cooper's Leatherstocking Tales.

"Who is that?" asks a surprised Percival.

"He is my companion, James." replies Martha. "Come, I want you to meet him. James will give you the knowledge that you need to satisfy your thirst for blood with animal blood."

The two young men, separated by almost two centuries, shake hands, and it is immediately obvious to Percival that James is more than just an apparition, as well.

James then speaks to Percival. "I, like Martha, was also a captive taken by the Shawnee into the Ohio country. I was able to escape and rejoin my English family after a five year period. During the time I was in captivity, I learned the Native American hunting skills that Martha has asked me to teach you. She believes that you are good and, in spite of what has happened to you, there is hope for you. I am sad for you because I know that in trying to cure your disease, the witch's spell has given you not only life, but immortality without a soul. Even our captors did not take our souls, they merely adopted them to replace the souls of lost relatives."

Percival now realizes that the reality of his new world is fully understood by his white captive friends from the 18th century. Fortunately for him, his heightened vision, hearing, strength, and speed will make him a very capable student for James to work with. This encounter at High Rock infuses Percival with a renewed hope. He now feels that he can seize more than just the moment. He can seize his immortality and, in conjunction with his new friends, utilize it as an opportunity to right the wrongs for which he knows he is responsible. Now he needs to put the fears that he has ignited in Sofia and Alexa to rest. He must confide in them. He will need their unconditional love and support in order to survive. He must tell them that he believes himself to be a vampire. He must make them believe that he will not harm them, and he must make them believe that they have his love and affection for the rest of their lives.

On their first hunting experience, it did not take James long to realize that Percival is no ordinary white woodsman. In his captivity, James had heard tales from other tribes about undead blood sucking humans with seemingly supernatural physical skills. When captured and burned, as their ashes drifted into the air, they turned into mosquitoes so that they could continue to feed on human blood. He had also heard similar tales about leeches and ticks. James was always careful to avoid their bites, and even more careful about killing them, for fear of retribution. After hearing these tales, James never looked at mosquitoes and other parasites in the same way, and now he wonders if he has not met one of these legends through his friend Martha.

Percival's stealth and speed are second to none that James has ever seen, even among his captors. His real fascination comes after

the catch, with the manner in which Percival literally rips into his

prey, tearing at their throats, and consuming their blood

in a frenzy, leaving the meat and furs behind for the other carnivores

of the Pigeon Hills. This is frustrating to James because he was

taught to make use of the entire animal out of reverence to Mother

Earth and in appreciation for all that she provides.

THE BLOODLINE

"Many of those who sleep in the dust of the earth shall awake. Some shall live forever, others shall be an everlasting horror and disgrace."
Daniel 12 1-3

The York County District Attorney, Ralph Fisher, kept his word.

After all, with everything that had happened two years earlier in

Rehmeyer's Hollow, how could he not follow up on the report of

this possible grave site within his jurisdiction?

Fisher, Frank Hoke, who notified him, and Bert Hoover, the land

owner who discovered the grave, went to the grave site with two

detectives from the District Attorney's office at about noon. The

warning "Beware" and the skull and crossbones were marked on the

tree as reported earlier by Frank Hoke.

The five men proceeded to exhume the grave, and

about four feet below the surface their shovels began to strike a wooden surface. When the dirt was cleared away, they had unearthed a primitive wooden coffin with a lid that had been tightly nailed down and wrapped in two chains, one at the head end and one at the foot end. District Attorney Fisher surmised that the chains were most likely used to lower the head and foot ends of the coffin into the ground and just left there.

The decision was made to transport the coffin to the Dunkard Church near Gnatstown for a preliminary examination and, if a body was found inside, then on to York for an autopsy and further investigation. Upon loosening the chains and opening the coffin lid, the five men were horrified to see the dead body of a young girl, believed to be in her mid to late teens, stretched out before them with her hands folded over her waist. She was extremely pale and did not look to have been dead very long, as she was not decomposing. She was fully clothed and had been placed in the coffin as though she would have been viewed prior to her burial by a funeral home. The left side of her neck had suffered a wound that resembled that of an animal bite of some sort. There was not a sign of much bloodshed on the body and there did not appear to be any other outward wounds.

District Attorney Fisher remarked that it seemed strange to him that there was no postmortem lividity, or that reddish-blue discoloration of the cadaver that occurs in the dependent portions of the body due to gradual gravitational flow of unclotted blood. There was no sign of identification other than a light loose fitting scarf on which the name Henrietta was embroidered.

As evening approached, Mister Hoke and Mister Hoover signed their statements for the District Attorney and returned to their respective homes. Photographs of the girl's body in the primitive coffin were taken and the District Attorney and one of his detectives also departed for York. They left the remaining detective at the church with the body until a hearse dispatched from York arrived to remove the corpse.

After a thirty minute wait, the detective on watch stepped outside the church for a cigarette and the hearse arrived. The detective and the hearse attendant went inside and picked up the primitive coffin and immediately put it back down, as it appeared too light to be containing the dead girl's body. They threw the lid of the coffin open and were terrified to see that the body was gone.

Upon receiving this information in York, District Attorney Fisher ordered his staff to say nothing of the incident to the press or the public for fear of creating chaos within the city and the surrounding countryside. When one of the detectives who witnessed the events asked him privately for his theory about the neck wound and the lack of postmortem lividity, he responded, "I don't know. I just don't know."

THE VICTIMS

"God is God of not the dead, but of the living; for Him all of them
are alive." Luke 20:38

Percival is not sure that he even remembers the girl's name. He

had seen her a few times as she walked by his home on her return

from the stores in Hanover. He is overcome with sorrow and shame

when Martha informs him of what he has done to this young girl.

Martha is holding him accountable for turning Henrietta into a

vampire. He is not even aware of what he has done and can

remember none of it, as he was in the process of his own

transformation at the time. Now Martha is challenging him to step

forward and take responsibility for the results of his turning of

Henrietta, and her subsequent turning of another teenage girl from

nearby McSherrystown.

Martha refreshes Percival's memory about his attack on Henrietta. How they had finally walked together and engaged in conversation, after only acknowledging one another countless times before when they had passed in the lane. They had always exchanged smiles and greetings and, to tell the truth, Percival finds the girl to be rather attractive. Her stature and shoulder length blonde hair remind him of his lost first love, Priscilla Kump. Perhaps it is this likeness that heightens his emotions and leads to his taking of her hand in his as they walk and talk, and the embrace in the woods that is followed by the bite on her neck.

He now remembers her melting in his arms with minimal resistance as he sucks her blood from the wound on her neck. He cannot stop. The taste of her blood drives him wild.

When she becomes weak and passes out, he begins to return to his senses. Then, in fear, he drags her body through the woods and disposes of it as best as he can, in a crude wooden box that he has hastily thrown together. He marks the site to attempt to ward off any

48

superstitious locals. Percival has no idea what he has set in motion in the Pigeon Hills and the Hanover area.

Henrietta Hostetter lives with her father, Henry, on a small farmette in the Pigeon Hills near the village of Gnatstown. Her mother had died when she was younger and her father is doing the best he can to raise his teenage daughter alone, with the help of a few ladies from the nearby Pleasant Hill Dunkard Church.

When Henrietta fails to return home, after leaving for the day to pick wild blueberries and raspberries along the trolley line, her father becomes irate. When she is then missing for a few more days, he goes insane and ravages the nearby countryside while he searches for Henrietta or her possible assailant.

The Gettysburg Compiler, June 21, 1930
Seek Vandal Breaking Tombstones With Axe in the Pigeon Hills
Vigilance Committee On Trail of Apparently Demented Man
Causing Damage
Damage Was Done Recently

A vigilance committee is searching for a man who wended his way down through the Pigeon Hills with an axe, chopping down trees, breaking tombstones, and causing havoc in general.

Apparently coming from the hills, the man passed through Moulstown, leaving a line of debris behind him, and came upon the

Mount Carmel Cemetery. Here he broke the top from a tombstone marking the grave of Levinah Moul, who was born July 17, 1826, and died January 15, 1909. The footstone at the grave of Sarah A., wife of Jacob H. Moul, was broken off by a stroke of the vandal's axe. Other stones were apparently struck at but resisted the blows of the axe, showing slight scars where struck.

Hacks Orchard Trees

Cherry trees belonging to Sam Bollinger were ruined. The mail box of John Sullivan, Moulstown, was cut from the post. Three fruit trees in the orchard of Edward Moul, Hanover, located near Moulstown, were cut. The fruit packing house was also broken into. Trolley stations from Jacobs' Mills to Hanover show the effects of the attack evidently made by the same man.

A resident in the hills is reported to have seen a man going down the road over the devastated route carrying an axe on the afternoon of June 15, at the time the deeds were committed. This man, Alfred Yohe, is said to have recognized the man carrying the axe.

It is thought that the man is demented. He was described as being a heavy-set man, about 30 years of age. It is understood that the York Railways Company intends to prosecute if the man is identified.

The York County authorities are notified, but remain mum on

their recent discovery, due to the puzzling wound and the condition

of the girl's body, not to mention her disappearance shortly after the

exhumation. They believe that they have a match for the missing

girl based on the scarf that was observed in the roughly made coffin.

But the authorities remain silent, not only because of the missing

body, but also because the photographs from the crude burial site revealed no image of the girl's body when they were developed by the district attorney's office.

The last the thing that the York County authorities want is a panic, especially since the sensationalism from the Hex witchcraft murder trial has recently appeared to be quieting down. They are doing all that they can to suppress the fact that the authorities at both the state and county levels are taking no action against the Pennsylvania German faith healing practitioners for fear of retribution, despite the mounting evidence against them. After what had occurred at Rehmeyer's Hollow, they were sure that there was some rational explanation for what they had just witnessed in the Pigeon Hills near Gnatstown.

The minute Percival entered the East Middle Street warehouse adjacent to the Fitz Water Wheel factory, he surveyed the crowd of teens gathered there looking for Henrietta Hostetter. As he began to move through the crowd, it happened.

"Percival Lorentz! What did you do to me?"

He rushed to Henrietta, taking her by the arm and leading her out of the room and into an adjacent abandoned office. He slammed the door as his friend, Don Weisensale shouted, "Hey P.J., did you finally get her to do it?" The room seemed to fill with laughter and then the noise faded as Percival attempted to quiet Henrietta, who was hysterical.

"What in the hell did you do to me? One minute we are walking in the woods starting to make out and, the next thing I know, I'm waking up in a box in the ground, being examined by five men who believe I'm dead. I just remained still until I could get away after they left me alone in the church."

Henrietta continued, "I could hear everything, but I couldn't move. I went into some sort of trance when the sunlight hit me as they opened the box. I felt much better when they brought me into the dimly lit church, so I ran away the first chance I got. What have you done to me? Did you rape me? Why do I crave blood so? I have so many questions. Then to make matters worse, Daddy went on a rampage and nearly did kill me. That is, after he tore up half of the Pigeon Hills trying to find me. I had to lie like hell about where I really was! He was big time pissed about me being gone for almost four days. I finally got off of the farm today after a big lecture from him about trust and then the women from church about keeping my virginity."

"Listen to me carefully, Henrietta. I did not ask for this either, and no, I did not rape you. I like you, I always have, you know that. We were just finding our way with one another when I was totally overcome with a crazy desire to feed on your blood. I just pulled your scarf away and bit you on the neck, and then I sucked all of your blood out of the wound. I could not stop. Your blood tasted so sweet. I thought I killed you, so I buried you in that wooden box over near Gnatstown.

Apparently when I was lost in the frenzy while feeding on your blood, I must have punctured my own lips and enabled you to consume some of my blood as well. I have learned that when a person has been drained of their blood to the point of death and they consume a vampire's blood, they also become a vampire. I've had the trance-like experiences, too, and I did not even remember that I had done this to you until I was informed by the Indian guide, Martha.

"It was then that I thought maybe I could have this curse reversed. I tried going back to see the powwow woman in Marietta, but all I found there was that her place on Front Street was boarded up. A few of the local people that I asked about her said that she has not been seen in weeks. One really strange woman remarked that she probably returned to her homeland to die and mumbled something about "water witches" from England, or the Netherlands, or someplace over there. I thought all the powwow doctors and witches were Germans.

"I also thought about going to my parents about this, but they are convinced by all of my outward appearances that I am fully recovered. And besides, my parents have more than enough to worry about with the Record-Herald looking like it might shut down.

"Two of my sisters, Sofia and Alexa, know better though, as I nearly dealt them the same fate as we suffer. Not long after that, I did this to you. I've spoken with both of them and they are keeping our secret and helping me to cover up our situation. They are also very frightened, but it seems to be getting better with time.

"I did not remember any of this until Martha, the Indian captive spirit, restored both my memory of these events and my conscience.

If it were not for her, I do not know where I'd be today. She is very mystical and can shape shift into a pigeon. I found out that the kind of pigeon that she becomes is called a Passenger Pigeon. They used to cover the Pigeon Hills, but now they are extinct. Ironically, the last one to die in captivity somewhere in Ohio was named Martha too. Now isn't that a strange coincidence?"

Henrietta listened carefully and began to sob. "I'm really scared, Percival. I have this very special friend, Anastasia Miller, from McSherrystown. Well, we're really close, if you know what I mean? I was telling her how I've been sucking the blood out of raw meat up at the farm, and chasing down small rodents and animals, killing them and drinking their blood, too. I told her that I felt weak and that I thought I needed to try some human blood pretty soon. I really didn't know what to do or who to talk to. Anastasia is a little crazy and wants in on everything, so she held out her arm and pointed to the inside of her elbow and said, 'Have at it.' Well, we did this a few times, and the last time I could barely stop, and now Anastasia is like us.

Now that you've told me how I got this way it explains what I inadvertently did to Anastasia. When I got carried away feeding from her arm and she went limp and collapsed into my arms I panicked. I thought I had killed her. I figured if I gave her some blood back she would recover. She seemed to have slipped into a deep sleep but she was still breathing alright. When she awoke, she said she felt weak and wanted some more of my blood. I bit my wrist and fed her some more. I thought I was helping her. I had no idea that I had done this to her.

I was too pissed off at you to even try to look for you to find out what the hell is going on. For that I guess I'm sorry, now that you tell me you have no idea what has happened to you either."

"Henrietta, I am so sorry about all of this. I'm not absolutely sure what we are. I've done some reading in the library, following up on what Martha and James have told me, and I believe that we have become some sort of vampires. Do you remember the book, Dracula, that our friends are all raving about, and the moving picture, "Nosferatu"? I've read part of the book and I've seen the moving picture over at the new State Theater. Well, they were written about monsters called vampires. I don't know if they are real or not, but we are. Also, Martha's friend, James, shared a Native American legend with me, and that was about people who craved blood like we now do. The Stoker guy who wrote the book about Dracula got a lot of this right, but religious stuff doesn't seem to bother me. I also read a small story called The Vampyre written by a guy named John Polidori way back in 1819. The librarian told me it was written as a part of a contest or something like that. Supposedly Polidori was involved with Mary Shelley, who wrote Frankenstein, Percy Shelley, and Lord Byron, and they decided to have a competition to see who could come up with the best horror story. Knowing what we know now, we sure could write one!"

"Percival, how can you joke about this? I've never read any books like that and, with Mama being gone, we don't have the money for me to see moving pictures. I can barely afford the fare money for the trolley most of the time. Percival, I'm afraid. What are we going to do about Anastasia? I do have an idea about how we can get fresh domestic animal blood. I know that you and I will be alright, but I'm worried about her. We need to get with her really soon. She is really getting anxious to try human blood and I'm afraid she will start an epidemic. I really like her a lot, but she does nothing in moderation. She told me she was coming to the warehouse this evening. We've got to find her now!"

Percival embraced Henrietta and replied, "We must stick

57

together. It is critical that we get with Anastasia right away and come up with a plan for our survival. We must keep our condition a secret or, from what I've read, our fate will not be pleasant."

He wiped the tears from Henrietta's eyes and again reassured her, saying, "I am responsible for all of this and I will not abandon you and Anastasia. I can assure you that I am in this with you for all eternity because, from what I've read, that will need to be the case."

At this point they left the old office and began to search the crowd to see if Anastasia had arrived. It did not take them long to find her surrounded by a group of Percival's counterparts, charming them with her beauty and wit. Henrietta manages to break Anastasia's spell on the boys and lead her away to be introduced to her neighbor, Percival Lorentz.

Anastasia took Percival's hand and looking into his eyes she quipped, "It is so nice to finally make your acquaintance, Percival. Henrietta has told me so much about you. It feels like I've known you forever, and now it seems that I will. Henrietta has had her eye on you for some time up there in the Pigeon Hills. Now I can see why."

Percival blushed and glanced at Henrietta who was standing there grinning. Henrietta then gave him a tap on the shoulder and whispered, "Just friends."

Percival realizes the moment that he is introduced to Anastasia, that there is hope that he might love again, despite the fact that his heart was broken by the termination of his lengthy relationship with Priscilla Kump. He had his eye on Priscilla since the first time he had seen her in the schoolyard at Saint Mary's in McSherrystown when he was but in the seventh grade. It was a classic small town junior high school romance. It started young and had become rather serious by the time Percival reached his junior year in high school. Priscilla's parents recognized the direction in which their daughter's relationship was heading and, with Priscilla being merely a freshman at Saint Mary's, they forbid her to see Percival any longer. He was crushed, and his subsequent transfer from Saint Mary's to Paradise Protectory and Agricultural School in Abbottstown had made matters even worse.

Prior to his turning, Percival had been lonely, and now with his transformation complete, this loneliness has been intensified along with all of the feelings that he is experiencing. The loss of Priscilla has devastated him and now the loss of his soul has placed him in a world of his own. It is a world that he shares with two young girls for whom he is ultimately responsible, one being Henrietta Hostetter and, the other, her friend and former voluntary donor, Anastasia Miller. When Percival first realized his fate, he immediately set about planning to extract his revenge by turning Priscilla so that she would again be his for all eternity; however, after this first encounter with Anastasia, the prospect for the future has all changed.

With the passing of the winter and early spring months, the need for the teens to gather at the old warehouse on East Middle Street has diminished. It is a blessing that the young apprentice at Fitz Water Wheel, Don Weisensale, was able to arrange for the use of the vacant warehouse as a place for the teens to safely gather and socialize out of the wintry weather. Their numbers had just become too great to linger for the evenings at the Texas Hot Lunch on Carlisle Street. The routine became one of meeting at the Texas, having a meal there, and then moving on to the YWCA, or congregating at the warehouse for music, dancing, and fellowship. The warehouse has become a healthy alternative when there are no programs on the schedule at the Hanover YWCA, which had opened back in 1920.

Weisensale, a senior at Hanover High School, has become a friend of Percival's through contact with him at the Record-Herald. They had met there when Don would stop by while running errands in his capacity as apprentice for the Fitz Water Wheel operation. Don had been able to get Percival some part time work over the summers as a shop helper at the company's factory on East Middle Street. It was Don who first referred to Percival as P.J. He had seen his full name on the brief application form as Percival Jeremiah Lorentz. Percival will come to use this nickname from time-to-time to alter his identity through the years.

Now that Percival has formally been introduced to Anastasia by Henrietta, the three of them have been able to separate from the crowd and discuss at length what measures they need to take in order to satisfy their hunger for blood. The shame and sorrow that

Percival is experiencing, as a result of the fate that he has cast on Henrietta Hostetter, is beginning to subside. Henrietta is much less furious about her situation and has changed her mind about her threats to take matters to the authorities. Percival has been quick to remind her that if she did so, they will all three, no doubt suffer a similar fate, with a stake driven through their hearts, decapitation, and cremation. He reminds the girls that he has been researching vampirism and that he has uncovered nothing about reversing the fate, only the Catholic Church's recommended methods to terminate it.

So now there are three young soulless creatures in the Hanover area forming a rather delicate alliance in order to merely survive. The one thing that they have in their favor is the hesitation that the local authorities exhibit, first-out of the fear that they will start a panic if they mention witchcraft or spells, and second-because of the fear of retribution from the witches and hexmeisters themselves.

The contact that Henrietta has established with a young man who works at the slaughterhouse on Chestnut Street, near the market, sounds as though it might be a workable solution for satisfying the girls' craving for blood. Percival is daily satisfying his hunger by using the hunting skills that he has developed after being schooled by James. It is nearly impossible for the girls to accomplish regular hunting with their different life styles. Henrietta has tried feeding on mice and rats that she has run down in the Pigeon Hills and the alleys of Hanover. She has also fed on an occasional squirrel. She likes the doves' blood the best, but they are just too difficult to run down. She is fast, but she still cannot fly.

Finally, as she fed on the human blood from Anastasia's arm, she lost control and turned her. It is a fate that she alone has endured at the hands of Percival, who drained nearly all of her blood when he was lost and alone in his transition before Martha's intervention. Now, the three of them find themselves soulless and mingling with the unsuspecting teens of Hanover, doing all they can to mask their plight and satisfy their hunger for blood. They have all agreed that the human victims would stop with them, although Anastasia made it very clear that she feels slighted.

Now, all that they needed to do was to further develop the plan to store the bottled animal blood that Henrietta is regularly receiving from her friend, Michael Wildasin. His family owns the slaughterhouse on Chestnut Street and the meat market on Broadway. It is easy for Michael to obtain the blood that is needed to sustain the girls. It is his job to funnel the blood from the severed throats of the animals to be slaughtered into bottles, to be used as blood meal for the roses grown in the greenhouses at nearby Cremer Florist. Henrietta had gathered and dried flowers and sold them to Cremer and was working there part time learning to arrange flowers. She was trying to help her daddy make ends meet on the farm. It was at Cremer Florist that she had met Michael. The girls had lied to Michael and told him that they were using it for fertilizer themselves, for their flower gardens at their homes, and that they applied it in its liquid form. As Michael has had his eye on Henrietta for some time, he was very happy to be of service to them.

It was near the end of this gathering that Percival and Anastasia had agreed to meet at Forest Park to roller skate. She told him that

she would be there with a group of students from his old school,

Saint Mary's in neighboring McSherrystown. He really wanted to

get to know her better and he even caught himself thinking, "Now

this would not be a bad way to spend eternity."

DOPPELGANGERS

"But the younger widows refuse: for when they have begun to wax wanton against Christ, they will marry; having damnation, because they have cast off their first faith."
1 Timothy 5:11-13

The trolleys are the social network of the late 1920's and early 1930's. The most popular line for the teenagers is the spur that transports them to join their friends at Forest Park, in south Hanover.

Anastasia so vividly remembers that evening, watching as Percival skated up to Maria from behind and gently took her hand. "It was supposed to have been my hand," Anastasia thinks. "He had come to the rink to meet with me." The memory of the way they exchanged no words, merely glances, as they glided around the rink hand-in-hand at Forest Park irks Anastasia to this day.

Maria should have acted surprised, but she did not. She should have resisted, but she did not. She could not pull her hand away, even though his grip was merely a relaxed one. To this day Maria cannot explain why. She had never met this gentle young man before, but somehow felt as though she has known him forever. How had he come to select her as she skated aimlessly around the rink that warm June evening?

The answer to this question is one that Maria will painfully have to deal with through the years to come. Percival knew that she was different the instant he took her hand and felt her warmth

After they skated to the side of the rink, he was even more stunned when he addressed her as Anastasia. They stopped and stood hand-in-hand. She gazed into his eyes and said nothing for a moment, and then she responded with a shy smile, "I'm not Anastasia. I'm her twin sister, Maria."

Percival should have realized this when he first took her hand and felt the warmth, but he remained captivated by her innocent face and her gentle receptive eyes. He knew immediately that she was "the one" that he wanted by his side for all eternity.

Make no mistake, Percival has been attracted to the physical beauty of Anastasia since they first met. In fact, the two of them had first embraced and kissed while at a small get together of Anastasia's friends near Smith's saw mill in Brushtown. They have been drawing closer to a romantic relationship. Percival has been able to ease some of the hostility that Anastasia has developed out of her frustration about what she has become and her unfulfilled craving for real human blood.

Anastasia knows that Percival is ultimately responsible for what has happened to both her and Henrietta, but also realizes that he, himself, is a victim. She was beginning to lose the anger over the loss of her soul, and was replacing it with a pleasure in using her newly acquired mental and physical abilities.

Of the three of these lost souls, Anastasia has become the most comfortable with her state of immortality. The affection that she was beginning to feel for Percival is now being channeled into anger and jealousy as she watches the blossoming romantic involvement between Percival and her twin sister, Maria. She vows to make Maria pay for this, but knows that she must be careful not to expose her condition.

Their meeting was completely innocent. There was no deception. There were no games played with zygosity. Percival is stunned. He had no idea. "I've seen Anastasia a few times, and now I cannot be sure it was always her."

Maria smiled. "Oh yes, you can be sure it was her. My being here tonight was purely an accident. I was just using up a leftover ticket so that our school would have enough kids to fill the trolley car. I got pressured into coming. I really do not like crowded places, but I do enjoy roller skating. Anastasia is on the go all the time. We are really different in that way. You haven't mentioned your name."

"Oh, I'm sorry. Percival, Percival Lorentz. I met your sister, your twin sister, through a mutual friend, Henrietta Hostetter. Do you know her?" He sees the quizzical look on Maria's face and begins to panic.

"What's up with those two?" she asks.

He safely takes the middle road and counters, "What do you mean?"

What he really wonders is how much does she actually know about her twin sister and Henrietta.

"Well, they sure have been spending an awful lot of time together lately. They seem real close, and they are always whispering about this or that. You would think that they are dating or something like that. You know what I mean? They are even touchy-feely! Wouldn't that be awful? I would not put anything past Anastasia! I don't pry though. We are not really that close, even though we look alike. Our parents are not even suspicious of anything she does. In their eyes, she can do no wrong. I guess that goes along with the seniority of getting here about five minutes before I did. You thought I was her, didn't you?"

Percival tells Maria the truth. "I've been with her a few times, you know, in the crowd where she was. I'll admit that. And I came here tonight to meet with her to kind of get to know her a little better."

Percival is struggling internally, trying to find the right words, because he is mystified by Maria's personality. "Now I must admit that I am confused, and so I have to ask you, is there a chance that we might see each other again? I know this seems awkward with me actually coming here to meet your sister, but it just feels right. Something about this night and our meeting just feels so right. I feel like this is the best thing that has happened to me in a long time."

He begins to think about having Maria for eternity and catches himself. "And now that I think back on it, I sort of remember seeing you twins jumping rope at recess. You were a few grades behind me when I was at Saint Mary's in McSherrystown. That was before I transferred to Paradise School.

Since you don't like hanging with the crowds, or being in the company of Anastasia, I can take the trolley to McSherrystown to meet with you."

Maria looks him square in the eyes. It is as though he is the one being compelled. "I would like that very much Percival Lorentz. Now I've got to run, so just call me. You can get the number from Henrietta."

She slips her hands from his and disappears in the direction of the trolley platform. As he stands there enjoying the memory of the past few moments, he rubs his mouth and delights in the aroma and taste that he senses from the hands that he has just held.

He is abruptly snapped back into his real world as Anastasia wisps by and shouts, "We'll see about this Percival Lorentz! I don't know what you think you are doing!" Percival now realizes that his meeting with Maria has touched off in Anastasia a resentment for the two of them that will bring dire consequences.

With the entrance of Percival into the lives of the Miller twins, the gap that exists between the girls has widened and deepened. When they arrived at home in McSherrystown, after watching Anastasia seething on the trolley, Maria was not a bit surprised when she heard, "Hey miss goody-two-shoes, what do you think you are doing spending the evening with the guy that I was supposed to meet at Forest Park? You're gonna pay for this, baby sister!"

Not assuming her usual silent tolerance of her sister's temper tantrums, Maria abruptly responded, "I'm not your baby sister! Anna is our baby sister!"

"Well, we will see who winds up with him in the end. You are really going to pay for this, sister! Just wait until you find out the truth about what you presume to be your knight-in-shining-armor. Wait until you see what he really is!"

Maria thought for a moment and responded, "Well, if he's that bad, why are you so interested in him?"

With that, Anastasia mumbled something else that ended with,

"You better say your prayers. You're gonna need them, Miss Saint!"

Young Anna yells, "Will you two be quiet!" and a temporary peace fell over the girls' bedroom as they settled under their covers.

While lying there, thinking about all that had happened earlier in the evening, Maria could not help but wonder what her twin sister was getting at when she remarked about "Seeing what he really is". Then she caught herself, "Oh well, that's Anastasia. I should know better." and drifted off to sleep.

Anastasia, on the other hand, remained awake and began to fantasize about ways that she could get revenge on Maria. She finally slipped into sleep thinking, "She will pay dearly for this."

Now herein lies the problem for Percival. He and Maria seem to have an attraction for one another. There appears to be no question about the feelings they possess for each other. The anguish that Percival is beginning to experience lies in the fact that he knows that unless Maria consents to him turning her, they only have a chance of being together until her death causes them to part.

This specter haunts him daily, along with the thought of his immortality and losing Maria at the time of her death. He just cannot imagine living forever without her by his side, but he is determined not to turn her without her expressing the desire for that to happen. If there is one thing that he has learned, it is that the taking of another's soul should never happen without their consent. His fate was accidental. Maria's fate must be voluntary. Percival wants no more victims.

Martha and James have helped him to regain his conscience. He fully understands the concept of free will despite the loss of his own soul. If a person is to be eternally wandering between heaven and hell, it must be by their own choosing.

How is he ever going to approach her about what he has become? How will she react? Will she be repulsed and reject him despite their feelings for one another? He has so many anxious questions.

While Percival sits in the shade on Broadway near the Fitz house, he observes a wedding party proceeding north on the old Abbottstown Pike. As the vehicles stream by he notices on the rear window of the bride and groom's car a sign with the first names of the newly-weds, "Catherine and Michael" with the quote, "Together Forever".

He thinks to himself, "Now, how can that be forever?

Didn't they just speak their vows, 'Until death do us part' or 'For as long as we both shall live'? The concept of parting at death certainly wipes out any truth about their being together forever."

With the assistance of Martha and James, Percival has come to a point where he can accept the reality of his own immortality, and do so while respecting other human life. His dilemma is accepting the mortality of his beloved Maria. He wants her by his side for all eternity. It is obvious to Percival that humans do not fully understand the meaning and concept of forever.

What is Percival to do about Anastasia? She is jealously awaiting the day of her sister's death and desiring to fill the void in Percival's life that will be left by Maria's passing. Anastasia has been turned by Henrietta and she knows that she is legitimately in Percival's bloodline. She is really his responsibility and he must come to realize that fact. All she has to do is patiently wait for the day of her twin sister's demise.

However, patience is not a virtue that Anastasia possesses. Can

Anastasia possibly do something to hasten this event without losing Percival herself? She is in the position now to be at his side forever. Why can't he see this and accept the facts as they are? She possesses all the attributes to make Percival a wonderful companion for all eternity. Why has he become so attracted to quiet and shy Maria? The fact that Percival first encountered Maria, when he was to be meeting with Anastasia at Forest Park, remains a source of frustration and anger for her.

Percival spots Henrietta and Anastasia at the Texas Hot Lunch on Carlisle Street and approaches them with caution. He is greeted sarcastically. "Well hello lover boy. Aren't you hanging out with Saint Maria this evening?" are the first words out of Anastasia's mouth.

"No, I wanted to catch up with the two of you and see how things are going with our present situation."

"Like you really care, you bastard!" blurts Anastasia.

Percival fires right back, "Well from what I hear, you are

hammering away at Maria every chance you get. What's up with all of your, 'Wait until you see what he really is' chatter all the time? Why don't you just go ahead and tell her, Anastasia? You are dying, excuse the expression, to put an end to the relationship that Maria and I have developed. Go ahead and kill that and, in the process, put an end to the three of us, as well. You are nothing but plain jealous of your twin sister! Can you feel it when the two of us are together, doppelganger? I hope you can! You and I had no commitment to one another. The only promise I made to you was for the meeting at Forest Park. For all intents and purposes, I kept that promise. Yes, I was initially attracted to you, and that led to my unintentional meeting with Maria. I can't help the way it turned out. Why can't you see that and just let it go? Why can't you and I, and Henrietta just work together and deal with our situation? That's all I want."

Anastasia is now in tears as she hears Percival out. "That's all you want! Well, let me tell you, Percival Lorentz, it certainly does not feel like that is all you want when you are with her, holding her, and kissing her. It drives me crazy. It should be me that you are holding, and me that you are kissing. What about that? Did you forget about that? You didn't seem to mind my company out in Brushtown that evening, now did you? But to put your fear to rest- no, I won't be the one to tell her about you. I'll leave that up to you as you put your hideous plan into action. You are a fool. I can be yours for all eternity. It's already done. It's all set up. And here you are, chasing that pathetic little angel, thinking that you will turn her and have her forever. I've got news for you, Percival, the only eternal life that Maria is chasing, is the one that she believes that Jesus Christ gave her through his death on the cross. Just you wait until you have to tell her what you really are. I'd love to be there to see her reaction to you, when you reveal yourself as the soulless creature that you really are. And I would also love to be there to see the look on your face, when she tells you what she really wants to be when she grows up. Go ahead, ask her that question, Percival! You think you know everything about your little darling Maria. Good

night, Percival. Sweet dreams you fool.

No, no wait, Percival! No, this is all wrong. You will see that

yourself in good time. I have no need to panic. I know my sister.

You will be all mine in good time. I just know it. All I have to do is

wait for you to realize the mistake that you are making. Percival,

thanks to what you've given me through Henrietta, I can and will

wait for you. After all, I have all the time in the world."

Percival hears her out and then just nods and departs. He wants

no further confrontation with Anastasia. As he walks to the trolley

station, he cannot help but wonder why Henrietta remained so quiet

during the course of this conversation. After all, was it not their

mutual quest for love and affection that had put this entire affair into

motion? And why did Anastasia suddenly execute the proverbial

"Jeckyl and Hyde" and appear to adopt a laissez-faire approach to

the entire situation after appearing so heated at first? So many

questions, and the three of them have all the time that they need to resolve their differences. But he knows that for his Maria, unless he can persuade her to allow him to turn her, there is the limit of a human life span.

He must carefully plan to reveal his true circumstance to Maria. Percival does not want to play games with Maria. He really does want her to know everything about him. He is terribly frightened that when she finds out what he is, she will terminate their relationship. He wants to be the one who tells her. He does not want her to hear it from Anastasia or Henrietta. But how and when do you break this kind of news to the one you love? He envisions himself holding her, looking into her eyes, and asking her, "How would you like it if I told you I could make it so that we are really together for all eternity? Not just this 'until death do us part' rhetoric, but really together forever. How would you like that?" He wonders how she will accept him when he promises her an endless future together, after telling her how it is that he can make that future a reality.

He is also troubled by Anastasia's remark about what Maria wants to be when she grows up. Was that just emotional talk, or does it have some substance? He must find this out, as well.

He has spent so much time with Maria in the towns of

McSherrystown and Hanover. It is time to take her to the Pigeon

Hills for a picnic. The site of the old Trappist Monastery will be the

perfect place to start the day, and he will make the revelation to her

at the beautiful site of High Rock.

As he rides the trolley to the outskirts of town, he feels much

better. He has a plan. Maria will certainly understand, and then she

will be his forever!

Percival cannot wait to put his plan into action. He calls Maria

by telephone and shares his idea about the picnic with her. He wants

to show her the Lorentz house on Hershey Hill, and then spend the

day escorting her around his beloved stomping grounds, the Pigeon

Hills. She is excited about the prospects of this day out and receives

her parents' blessing for the date. It is all set-a formal meeting with

Percival's parents and sisters, and then a wonderful day together in

the woods.

Maria can hardly wait and, when it is all confirmed, she teases him saying, "My sister keeps making sarcastic remarks about us and she always ends with 'Wait until you find out what he really is'. I can't for the life of me figure out what it is that she means. How could she possibly know some big secret about you? She has not even known you that much longer than I have, has she? Percival Lorentz! Is there something that you haven't told me about yourself? Are you keeping some deep and dark secret from me? C'mon Percival, I really want to know."

Percival answers quickly and puts her off stating, "As we continue to see each other, I'll gradually tell you everything about myself, I promise. You have not even told me what you want to be when you grow up either." They both laugh and return to discussing the next time they will be together, for a picnic in the Pigeon Hills.

THE REVELATION

"There is no fear in love, but perfect love casts out fear. For fear has to do with punishment, and whoever fears has not been perfected in love." 1 John 4:18

What a beautiful late October day it is. The Pigeon Hills are ablaze with a myriad of autumn's finest colors. A chill remains even though it is now late morning, and the aroma of wood smoke from the great fireplace in the house on Hershey Hill fills the air. Maria and Percival enjoy a wonderful opportunity to sit in the parlor and chat with his parents, Jeremiah and Genevieve. Sofia, Alexa, and Sarah all greeted Maria warmly. She had met the two oldest girls before, and is noticeably nervous sitting there with his parents for the first time.

She feels much more relaxed when Jeremiah remarks, "We cannot tell you how happy we were when we learned that Percival is seeing a good Catholic girl from McSherrystown. We are delighted, are we not, Genevieve?"

Percival's mother nods and smiles. It is obvious that she

understands Maria's uneasiness and she remarks, "Let's let them get on with their day's adventure. Remember, dear, the hours of daylight are growing shorter."

The two older girls remain in the parlor for a short time before leaving. Sarah makes off rather quickly, giggling as she runs out to rejoin her doll collection in her room.

When the older girls reach the upstairs hall by their bedrooms, Alexa takes Sofia by her arm and asks, "Do you think she is safe? I know they have been together a great deal, but not alone like they will be today. There have always been people nearby. I'm scared for her after what happened to us, Sofia."

Sofia hugs Alexa. "I understand your concern for Maria. I trust he will do nothing to harm her. I think he seems like his old self since he met her, don't you? Remember when he took the two of us to that little grove by the spring not too long after he had nearly attacked us both? He explained in detail what he has learned about what has happened to him, what he has become. He went on to tell us about the passenger pigeon we both saw and the Native American captives who helped to restore his conscience. I believe he genuinely trusts the insights that Martha and James have given him. Now we must trust him."

84

Alexa would not let go of Sophia. "I'm still worried about what he might do. He's got to tell her about this, too. What if she does not accept it and he loses his control over his ability to crave her blood. Then what? I'll tell you what! Then our brother again becomes the murdering monster that he really is!"

"What are the two of you arguing about up there? It has your younger sister upset. Come down here right away and bid your brother and Maria farewell."

The girls do as they were told. Percival and Maria set out on foot over the path that would take them to the north face of the Pigeon Hills and the old Trappist Monastery, their first stop. They did not hear the discussion with his sisters after the great wooden door to the Lorentz house had closed.

"What in the world were the two of you jabbering about up there? Sarah ran in here and said she is afraid of monsters, and was worried about her brother and Maria alone in the woods. I know it is close to Halloween, but you have to be more careful around her. She is still so young."

Sophia was quick to respond. "Mother, please forgive us. We were bantering about whether or not Percival and Maria would remain serious enough to ever be married, that's all it was. We were

85

talking about how he appears to be so madly in love with her and that he is always chasing her around."

Alexa counters, "Well, what do you think, mother?"

"Oh listen to the two of you! You are both too young yourselves to be thinking about marriage, anyone's marriage! Now run along and make sure your little sister understands that she has nothing to fear."

Alexa glances at Sofia as if to say "Oh, sure.", and they again retreat to the upstairs to ease little Sarah's worries.

When Percival and Maria arrive at the old monastic site, they sit together on an ancient stone bench near the abandoned well. The brick pathways through the garden are still visible, as much of the overgrowth has been killed off by the early autumn frosts.

He takes her hands in his and says, "Well, what do you think of this place? Peaceful, isn't it. I come here often just to sit and think. I thought you would like it here. It's kind of a spiritual place, isn't it?"

Reaching into his pocket, he continues, "I want you to have this." He pulls out an old crucifix that had, no doubt, been dropped there and lost by one of the monks who had worked in the very garden where they now sit. "It's made of silver, and the wooden inlay is no doubt from a sacred relic, maybe from the cross of Christ, or something like that. Who knows? Look closely on the back, down at the bottom. You can see the word "German" etched into the silver. I know how important the Catholic faith is to you and I want you to have this to remind you of me when you pray."

"Oh Percival, it is beautiful and means so much to me. Your thoughtfulness is beautiful, as well. I will always remember this moment and cherish this gift. How can you bring yourself to part with it? It is so beautiful! Just look at it! Look what Jesus did for us! He died on this cross and conquered death so that we may have eternity."

"While it remains, to me, a treasured find among my other Indian and Colonial relics, I know that it will have far deeper meaning for you, Maria."

After a quick embrace and kiss, they enjoy the light picnic lunch that Maria had prepared for them, topped off with fresh well water from right there at the ruins of the old Trappist Monestery. The first segment of this day has been enchanting, almost magical, perhaps even closer to spiritual.

As the young couple make their way over the path to the northeast and High Rock, the discussion begins about their futures.

87

Percival is getting very anxious as Maria begins to question him about his feelings.

"It did not seem like you ate very much back there. Was it my preparation of our lunch? Mama says I'm improving in the kitchen, but then she always says I still have a long way to go."

"Oh no, it was nothing like that. I think your apple turnovers are the best that I've ever tasted. I just try not to overeat, you know. Wait until you see the view from High Rock. You can see all the way over to my new school on the other side of Abbottstown. It is a beautiful clear and crisp day. We will be able to see our way to forever on this day."

"So, tell me, what is it that you want to be when you grow up-A nurse, a teacher? C'mon tell me. Anastasia says I'll really be shocked when you answer this question. What's the big secret?"

"Well, I'm not ready to tell you yet, Percival Lorentz! Not until you tell me why that wild twin sister of mine keeps saying that I will never be able to stand you when I find out what you really are. I cannot for the life of me imagine what could possibly be that awful. It's your turn Percival. You tell me first!" Then all is quiet for what seems like an eternity as they walk hand-in-hand toward their destination, High Rock.

When they do arrive, they immediately walk arm-in-arm out to the very edge. Maria takes a deep breath and sighs, "Oh my God! This is perhaps the closest I've ever felt to my God. I feel that we are so near to Him right now." She is holding the crucifix in her hand and she kisses it. She then turns to Percival and kisses him. She notices a tear running down his cheek. "What is it? What could possibly be making you appear saddened?"

"I have memories of this place, that's all." He takes her hand and leads her to sit upon the rock that he was once led to himself by Martha, after she had intervened and stopped him from taking his own life.

He thinks in silence. "Where is Martha now? There are no passenger pigeons any more. Why can't she appear now and make this easier? She could make what I am about to reveal to Maria believable. Martha could do this in a way that would not risk frightening her and driving her away. I must do this now. I can't put it off any longer." They sit there without a word.

Maria gently asks, "What are you Percival? What does Anastasia mean? I know she wants you. I know the two of you were together before you met me. I was there at Smith's party in Brushtown but I remained in the shadows. I saw the closeness that the two of you were developing. You appeared to get along so well. It was as though the two of you had something in common. It looked like there was an inseparable bond between the two of you. I also know it was Anastasia that you planned to meet at Forest Park.

It just felt so right as we were skating, so I did not say anything. The way this has worked out is like a dream for me, but Anastasia makes it sound more like it is going to be a nightmare. Please tell me, Percival. I need to hear this. I need to understand what she means. Tell me, and then I'll tell you what I've always wanted to be when I grow up."

Percival stands up right in front of Maria and takes both of her hands in his. The time has come. He begins, "Do you believe that we can attain immortality?"

"Of course." she answers. "Jesus died on the cross so that we might have eternal life with him after we die. You believe that too, don't you, Percival?"

"I did, I mean I do. Well, for most people, but I do not believe that is the case for me anymore."

Maria looks puzzled. "Well, just what do you mean by that? Jesus died on the cross for all of us. He has overcome death. If we believe in Him and carry out his works, if we are doers of his word, then He will have a place for us in heaven."

"I understand that but, you see, something terrible has happened to me and I am now trapped between heaven and hell. Some people call my kind "the damned" because of the way some of us live. I can have neither heaven nor hell, and I am destined to live on this earth forever."

Maria tries to pull her hands away and Percival holds them tightly. For the first time she feels his strength. She cannot pull away. "Let go of me! Percival, you are frightening me with this talk. I want to leave. I want to go home. What are you? What are you trying to tell me? Are you a vampire? Have you killed anyone? Oh my God, help me! Are you one of those vampire creatures? Oh my God, you are!"

"Maria, I will never hurt you. Before we leave here, Maria, you need to tell me that you believe that I would never do anything to harm you. You must trust me. I'm finished with human victims. That is the most important thing you can ever do for me. Please trust me and tell me that you will give me a chance to meet with you again. You need to give me the opportunity to tell you the whole story. After that, if you feel it is necessary, we will part and go our separate ways. But remember this, Maria. If we part, then I will

91

truly be damned to live my life for all eternity without you. For me, Maria, you are the one that I want to be with forever."

Percival releases Maria's arms and instead of running away, she just sits there and cries.

"You are not afraid of me, are you?" whispers Percival.

"No, I was when it first dawned on me what you were trying to tell me. I'm still really confused, but I realize that if you have not killed me by now, you mean what you say, and I can trust you. It's just scary, that's all. I know from what other kids have said that vampires feed on human blood in order to live They have said a bunch of other stuff about vampires, too. But from knowing you the way I do, I'd say some of it isn't true. They got their ideas about vampires from books and movies. My God they're-I mean you're, real! I don't know what to believe. Do you kill people?"

"I've killed one other person. I know that you know her and she is now like me."

"Who is she? It's not my sister, is it?"

"Well, not directly. It is Henrietta Hostetter."

"Oh my God, and she did this to Anastasia?"

"Yes, Maria, Henrietta turned your sister, but she was not forced into it."

"I knew it. I knew she was up to something the way she kept telling me that I would never want to stay with you when I found out about this."

"Anastasia was sharing her blood with Henrietta, trying to be a good friend and help her out. Well, it is really hard for us to stop feeding once we start, especially when we are new. Henrietta lost control and turned her. She could not help it. We get really weak without fresh blood, even animal blood works for us. That is what we are feeding on now. It is just the three of us, and we are finding our way without hurting anyone else. Please, you've got to keep this to yourself."

"But how do you control yourself around me when we hug and kiss and do things like that?"

"Believe me, it isn't easy, but I've had the right kind of help. And while I am still a soulless creature, I have regained my conscience. I do know right from wrong."

"Maria, will you help us to protect our secret? Even with no prospect of salvation, I still want to live a good life and remain responsible in assisting Henrietta and Anastasia because I am totally responsible for what has happened to them."

Maria wipes her eyes and pulls Percival close to her and looks into his eyes. "I need some time. Do you understand that?"

"Of course I do, Maria."

"Percival, since I met you, I was beginning to reconsider all of my dreams and plans about my future. I saw us together forever in my dreams-with a house and a family. Now I don't know what to think or what to believe."

"Maria, take all the time that you need. Your faith is strong and we can still fulfill your dreams. I share those dreams with you, Maria. Since we met, what plans did you have that you mentioned you had to reconsider? Did you have a previous love?"

"Oh, no, Percival. Until I met you, I had planned to go into the convent."

LIVING FOREVER

"Everyone who lives and believes in me will never die."
John 11:26

"The night is far gone, the day is near. Let us then lay aside the works of darkness and put on the armor of light." Romans 13:12

Percival has never felt more insecure in his entire life. No words are exchanged as he and Maria make their way to the trolley station for her return to McSherrystown, following their afternoon together in the Pigeon Hills. "Where will it go from here?" he wonders, as they wait for the arrival of the trolley.

He can sense the gravity of the situation. He can hear her rapid heartbeat and the sound of the blood gushing through her carotids. He can feel that she is still quite emotional after learning of his condition, despite the fact that she said she does not fear him.

This is not the everyday teenage love affair. Here are two young people who had really begun to feel a strong emotional bond developing between them. Now it appears that their future together has reached a crossroad.

Then suddenly, and to Percival's surprise, Maria takes his hand and kisses him on the cheek saying, "I am confused by what you told me about yourself today, and I will see you again because I want to know more. And I promise you this, I will not abandon you. I will never do that."

Despite the anxiety and despair that Percival is feeling, at least he now holds a faint glimmer of hope that maybe, just maybe, he and Maria may be able to build some sort of a future together. With that, he kisses her hand and she boards the trolley for McSherrystown.

Percival shouts, "I'll get word to you, Maria!"

She nods and shouts back, "I'll be waiting!" The trolley pulls away into the late autumn evening.

As Maria lies in her bed reflecting on the day's events, Anastasia whispers from across the room, "Well, sister dear, how was your afternoon with your knight-in-shining-armor? I bet you don't see him quite in the same light now, do you?"

Maria does not respond. She smiles to herself as she begins to think of ways that she might be able to help Percival. That is Maria, always trying to be of help to a friend in need. It is her nature. It is the way she was raised in the Catechism. It is the right thing to do.

However, she does wonder if Percival will still feel the same way about her, after he has time to think about her reaction to him when he revealed his true fate. She hopes it is so, and she prays it is so. She silently recites the Lord's Prayer as she drifts off to sleep… "Thy will be done, on earth, as it is in…"

For the first time in their relationship, it is Percival who deliberately goes in search for Martha. He walks his favorite arrowhead fields near the southern base of Hershey Hill. There is no sign of her anywhere; she is nowhere to be found. He knows that the Passenger Pigeons are extinct, but he also knows that this particular one is special. If he ever needed her wisdom and advice, it is now.

It dawns on him to move into the wooded area where she first shape shifted from the pigeon to her persona as the white Native American captive that she really is. He has looked for her at the ruins of the old Trappist Monastery and at High Rock to no avail. If she is again going to intervene on his behalf, he believes it might well be at the place where they had their first encounter.

Sure enough, he has barely had the time to catch his breath and sit on a log, and there she is, perched on the rock outcropping, spreading her wings. Before he knows it, the teenage white girl in Native American garb is seated there and the pigeon is nowhere to be found.

"Hello, Percival. You seem perplexed. It appears to me that you have handled the situation about as well as you could have. You appear to have a grasp on your free will and the choices you make after determining right from wrong. But your emotions-you must learn to control your emotions, particularly with regard to love."

"What do you mean?" he asks.

"I am referring to this passion that you have for entrapping Maria here in this world with you for all eternity. Isn't that really selfish?"

"But I love her!"

"Listen carefully to me, Percival. I understand your love for this girl, and she is very worthy of it. But I must forewarn you that she has a very strong commitment to her faith, and to her Savior, Jesus Christ. For you to attempt to drive a wedge into this relationship will be a fatal mistake, and I know that your life will be one of eternal emptiness and misery if you do."

"Are you saying that I should abandon my feelings for her? Now, how do you expect me to do that? You know how I feel about her."

"You must put her first, ahead of any of your own self interests. You have asked her to trust you, and she does. Now you must trust her. Percival, this young girl may hold the key to the reclamation of your soul.

"I have been able to help you with matters of conscience. It is Maria who may be able to help you with matters of the soul. She has said that she will not abandon you. Believe her, listen to her, and most importantly, trust her. Do not focus on your own happiness, but on hers.

"It will be in allowing Maria to tend to the welfare of her soul that you ultimately end up on the path to reclaiming your own. There are many who believe that when a man marries a woman, he loses his soul to her. Your soul has already been taken from you, and turning Maria will accomplish nothing but the creation of another soulless creature. Is that what you really want for her?

"You were raised in her faith. While you feel rejected by your God, you have not turned your back on Him. You are not like those of your kind who are considered "damned" by some of the researchers and fiction writers of your time. You know what is right, and you know what is wrong. If you are to ever join Maria for all eternity, it must be on her terms and, more importantly, on God's terms. I admire the fact that you have continued to attend Mass, now you must learn to pray again. Maria will help you.

"I must be gone now. I will always be nearby, and will meet with you at this place whenever you need me. Remember, Percival, God knows all of the secrets of our hearts."

Percival hangs his head and mumbles, "I would die a thousand deaths for her. Maybe I was really cursed the day I laid eyes on her."

Martha gazes down at this poor wretched creature and says, "The Lord be with you, my brother."

And without even thinking, Percival responds, "And with your spirit."

Percival is determined to get this right and, after this meeting with Martha, he is now even more determined to make the right choices in maintaining his relationship with Maria. He must get a message to her.

He proceeds to Cremer Florist and purchases a single long stemmed rose. He then writes a brief message to Maria and copies Shakespeare's Sonnet 29 onto a card.

He delivers it to her address in McSherrystown, and when no one is home, he leaves it out in the cold on the front porch. When Maria picks it up, the late fall temperatures have blackened the rose, but that does not matter to her. It reads, as follows:

My dearest Maria, How I long to be with you. I would like nothing more than to meet with you and spend another afternoon at High Rock. I know we have much to talk about. I'll phone you and we'll get permission from your parents to go on another picnic.

With love, Percival

Sonnet 29

When in disgrace with fortune and men's eyes,
I all alone beweep my outcast state,
And trouble deaf heaven with my bootless cries,
And look upon myself and curse my fate,
Wishing me like to one more rich in hope,
Featur'd like him, like him with friends possess'd,
Desiring this man's art and that man's scope,
With what I most enjoy contented least;
Yet in these thoughts myself almost despising,
Haply I think on thee, and then my state,
Like to the lark at break of day arising
From sullen earth, sings hymns at heaven's gate;
For thy sweet love remember'd such wealth brings
That then I scorn to change my state with kings.

Maria, Shakespeare understands. Love, Percival

Jeremiah and Genevieve give Percival their permission to entertain Maria again for a Sunday visit to the Pigeon Hills, despite the fact that the house is in disarray as they are packing for the family's move to York.

The Hanover Record-Herald will be closing soon with its final edition leaving the presses on November 4, 1930. Jeremiah has accepted an offer from his neighbor, J.W. Gitt, to work as a section editor for his Gazette & Daily in York. Percival will finish his schooling in residence at Paradise and the Lorentz girls will enroll at Saint Mary's School in York.

Maria's parents also gave their consent for the picnic. The get-together is finally scheduled. Percival can hardly wait.

The day is beautiful. Percival is having a very difficult time convincing Alexa that she really does not want to accompany him and Maria on their walk and picnic at High Rock. When Genevieve sees what is happening, she chuckles and reminds Alexa that she is needed at home to help pack and prepare for the move to their new home in York.

They are not together at High Rock for any period of time before Maria breaks the ice when she asks, "How did you get this way?"

Percival thinks for a moment and then replies, "You'd better sit down. This may take a while." Maria now sits comfortably on the same rock where she had experienced so much tension only a week before.

"Well, it started when I was told by our doctor that I have this premature aging sickness. There is no known cure for it, so out of desperation my father took me to see a lady known as the River

Witch of Marietta, over across the river in Lancaster County. This woman chanted some things and had me recite some prayer type of sayings, and then I had to have blood drawn out and replaced with blood from Sofia and Alexa.

"During one of those blood changing sessions, I remember lying there on the table. I had a feeling like I was floating up off of the table in a double of my body while my actual body remained on the table. It felt like I was dreaming this, all the while I seemed to be floating toward this bright light which also seemed to keep rising and out distancing me. It kept appearing to be farther and farther away from me, and it kept getting smaller and smaller all the time. Well, suddenly it went pitch black. The double of my body that felt like it was floating came crashing down and, went back into the body on the table.

"I woke up, and when I saw Sofia's blood dripping down through that clear tube, I just pulled it out of my arm and started drinking it. Since that day I have had an insatiable appetite for blood, particularly human blood.

"You have no idea how hard it was for me in those earlier days, when the craving for human blood was at its highest level. It was on one of those days that I could not control myself and I turned

103

Henrietta. I also attacked Sofia and Alexa and, if it was not for Martha stopping me, I very well may have turned them or maybe even just killed them.

"I am still not sure how all of this works or what I really am. I'm slowly piecing it together while I try to help Henrietta and your sister to deal with it, as well. We all agree that we do not want any more human victims. I now feed only on animal blood. Henrietta and your sister feed on slaughterhouse blood. It is working for us, but you still would not believe how much I would just love to taste your blood. I can smell it. I can hear it running through your veins and arteries."

He saw that Maria was starting to tense up a bit. "Have you heard enough?"

"No, I'm alright. It's just so scary and creepy that something like this can really happen. But I believe that you are demonstrating that just because you have become a vampire does not mean that you have to become a monster. Go on."

"Well, there really isn't much more to tell you about how it happened. I do believe that we are a species of vampire. That much I do believe. I also found out that the Catholic Church believes that we exist. In November of 1215, the Catholic Church officially recognized the existence of vampires during the Fourth Lateran

Council in Rome. God may be all merciful, but throughout its

history, the Catholic Church has not been very merciful to our kind.

God may be, but the church has not been."

"Percival, I really like you a lot. I mean, I love you. In spite

of what has happened to you, I still do. I hope this doesn't hurt you,

but I really do not want to be like you. I was born, I want to live a

good life, and I want to die and go to heaven. In that way, through

Jesus Christ and the sacraments, I will live forever. I know because

of your Catholic upbringing, that you understand how that works. I

simply cannot imagine not having my soul. I believe that your soul

is out there somewhere, and that you are not a damned person or a

demonic creature. You are suspended on this earth in some state that

may be like a Purgatory, or something like that. You are not saved,

nor are you condemned. You are trapped without your soul between

heaven and hell. I suppose depending on the paths you choose, it

could be for all eternity. Even with the life that you have been

given, my faith leads me to believe that your soul may be reclaimed

if you live in the proper manner-loving both God and your fellow

man. I believe to the depths of my soul that our God is all merciful

and that no sin is unforgivable."

"Maria, I admire the depth of your faith. It is just so hard for me to accept that I will go on living forever after you die. That thought haunts me. I feel like it is a judgment of hell on this earth, not having you for all eternity. I told Martha that maybe I was really cursed the day I first laid eyes on you."

"Percival, maybe the answer lies in you renewing your commitment to our faith. I mean, you said you went to see a witch, but are they not also referred to as "faith healers"? Wasn't prayer involved in you treatments? Maybe faith is still the answer. You've been going to Mass, but have you been to Confession?

" We have this really nice young priest at Saint Mary's, Father Jonathan Kealy. He is very understanding and does a great deal for the teenagers in our parish. In fact, he organized the skating party at Forest Park the night that we met. Maybe you should talk to him in the confessional. Our Catechism teacher told us that it is the confessor's obligation to keep absolutely secret what a person has told him in Confession. She said it is called the "seal of Confession" or the "sacramental seal." In a new book I'm reading called Living Forever, it says that never in the whole history of the Catholic Church has a priest been known to break the seal of the confessional. Maybe if you renewed you Baptismal Vows and made a Confession, there's a chance you could reclaim your soul. Don't you think it would be worth a chance?"

"Maria, are you absolutely sure that you do not want to join me in this world for eternity? I do not know for sure what will happen if I go into the confessional, but I do know the result if you let me turn you. We will be together forever. I know you have had to think about that."

Maria begins to cry. "Percival, if we are going to have any kind of a relationship into the future, please do not ever ask me to do that again. It upsets me."

He hears Martha's voice echoing in his head, "Trust her. Trust her. Her heart belongs to Jesus and her soul belongs to God. Her faith has already given her the opportunity for her immortality."

Percival sits quietly and just gazes at the object of his affection. Maria sits equally as quiet and looks into his eyes as they hold each other's hands. In the silence he comes to realize that he is going to have to give Maria his complete trust. He remembers being told one time that the first time you fall in love, it changes your life forever, and that no matter how hard you try, the feeling never goes away. It stays with you forever. Thinking back to Priscilla Kump, he knows that he could not say that Maria was his first love, but no matter what he will do, it is Maria who will stay with him forever.

"Maria." He breaks the silence. "I promise I'll never ask you to turn again. And, I'll see your friend, the priest. When can we do it? Will you go to the church with me and show me where to go? I don't want to go when it's crowded. I'm afraid."

Maria hugs him and replies, "Of course I'll go with you. I told you that I will not abandon you. I meant it."

She finds it hard to believe that Percival, through no effort of his own, has become one of the most feared and powerful creatures on the earth, and yet he admits that he is afraid. She thinks to herself, "Fear of the Lord is probably a good place to start."

"Confession is next Saturday evening. We can meet at my house on North Street and walk over to Saint Mary's from there. I'll show you where Father Kealy hears Confession. His confessional is right in the back. You've been to our church, you know where I mean. It has a booth on either side and the priest's room is in the middle. You'll be fine. If anyone can help you, it'll be Father Kealy. I just know it."

When they depart from High Rock this time, they again have a plan to meet the following weekend. Only this time, Maria is the one who is worried as to whether Percival will go through with their planned meeting.

Percival's family had relocated to York that week and the big house on Hershey Hill was vacant. He convinced Maria to make her way into Hanover and then he lured her out of town and up to the empty house.

His intentions are pure, and he does nothing to compromise Maria's chastity or the state of her soul. All they talk about is the anticipated success of tomorrow's visit with Father Kealy.

He feels so safe and secure in her presence. They sit on the hearth and Percival manages a small fire to keep the chill out of the air. The room is illuminated by a single candle, as the power has been turned off. To say it is enchanting would be understating the atmosphere, and they are both captivated by what they have incidentally created.

They are just settling into a very comfortable and romantic position with Maria seated on Percival's lap, when there is a vicious pounding on the front door. They are both startled. Percival jumps up and runs to the door with the fireplace poker in his hand. He throws the door open and there stands a frantic Henrietta Hostetter.

"Percival, you need to take her and get out of here! Anastasia found out that you two met in town and she is in a rage. She said

that she could feel everything that is going on between the two of

you. She said that she knows you headed up here and that she

intends to put an end to both of you the only way she knows she

can."

"And how is that?" asked Percival.

"I think she intends to burn the place down. She knows that fire

will kill you and she does not care about her sister. Everybody

knows that your daddy took your family to York when the paper

closed last week. I'm warning you. She's coming. I'm getting out

of here because I don't want her to know I got here first and told

you. Hell, she's crazy right now. She'll try to kill me too! I'm

going up the road to the farm. Get out of here!"

Percival takes Maria and scampers up a trail to the top of the

southern slope of the Pigeon Hills. From there they watch in

horror as the great mansion burns to the ground.

The authorities dismissed the fire as accidental. They said it was

probably the result of vagrants being careless with candles or the

fireplace. They wouldn't dare mention any suspicion of phantoms or

vampire activity. There had been a touch of that again with the

recent passing of Halloween and, with the anniversary of the Hex murder approaching, the last thing they needed on their hands was a terrified populace. The chief-of-police routinely warned others after the fire, not to publicize when homes were going to be vacant because, with the cold weather setting in, the homeless tend to break in and seek shelter.

Anastasia read the chief's warning in the paper and just grinned. By now she knew that she had missed them, but she was happy that she had given them a good scare.

Late Saturday afternoon, Percival arrives on the trolley and walks down North Street to Maria's house. He is greeted by her parents and her younger sister, Anna. Anastasia is nowhere to be found, of course, and that is perfectly alright with the both of them. They exchange niceties with Maria's parents, who have to repeatedly quiet Anna for teasing her sister about having a boyfriend.

They bid their farewells and walk down North Street and around the corner onto Third Street. There stands Saint Mary's. It looks more like a Gothic cathedral to Percival than a parish church. He is beginning to feel a bit scared again. Maria senses this, and as they reach the steps, she takes his arm and says, "C'mon now. Calm down. You are doing the absolute right thing being

111

here."

Percival squeezes her hand. "I'm glad you're with me, especially after last night. How could she?"

"Don't worry about that right now. Think about what you are going to say to Father Kealy."

They climb up the large set of steps closest to Main Street, enter through the large wooden doors, and reach the rear of the church. It is a massive brick structure, built in 1901. It is very dimly lit and the flames from the vigil candles dance and flicker in the front behind the Communion railing.

"I'll go first, so I'll be waiting for you right outside the confessional when you are finished, and then we can go and kneel and say our penance together. I want to light a vigil candle before we leave church. I save my allowance and I always light a candle in memory of my grandparents."

Percival watches as Maria enters the confessional to the left of the Priest's center door. The door closes behind her and he can hear nothing. He stares at the dark wooden cross that stands over the door behind which the Priest sits. It is imposing.

All of the sudden, the other door to the right of the Priest's opens and a woman exits and kneels down to do penance. The next person in line then enters. Maria is now making her Confession.

Percival thought, "How can someone as faithful as she even have anything to confess?" His love has grown to affectionate admiration. "She is so beautiful on the outside." he thought, "She must be immaculate on the inside."

His warm thoughts are abruptly interrupted as Maria exits her confessional with folded hands. It is his turn. She nods her head toward the confessional door and he steps in and closes the door.

It is musty and dark inside the confessional. He can hear nothing. Then in the distance he hears the door to the window on the other confessional slide closed. Immediately, he hears the door in his confessional slide open. He can barely make out the silhouette of the Priest on the other side of the screen. He can see the priest's hand move as he blesses him.

"The Lord be in thy heart and on thy lips, that thou mayest truly and humbly confess all thy sins, in the name of the Father, and of the Son, and of the Holy Ghost. Amen."

Hearing this, Percival makes the sign of the cross for the first time since he was beset by the witch's spell gone bad. Having made the sign of the cross he then says, "Bless me father, for I have sinned. It has been one year since my last Confession. I have not

113

received Holy Communion since then. I am a vampire."

AUTHOR'S NOTES

This begins on a rainy Monday morning in May of 2012 when I was supposed to be cleaning up the mess that remains upstairs from the two bookcases that mysteriously fell over, dumping their contents on the floor of the computer nook. In reality, there is no mystery here. The ghost of little 10 year old Nellie V. Wagaman descended from her resting place on South Mountain and created this mess after a second visit to her obscure grave site yielded no effort on my part to connect her to the proper Wagaman family line.

Instead of working on the bookcase mess, I opted for the end of the _Dark Shadows: The Haunting of Collinwood_ DVD and a quick run to the Gettysburg outlets for a couple of slices of pizza and a Diet Coke. While sitting there in the food court I, a former school administrator, was reminded of my days on cafeteria duty as a large

115

group of middle school students on a field trip were noisily taking their lunch break under the watchful eyes of their accompanying chaperones. I saw all of those potential pop culture customers just waiting to add the *Lost Soul of the Black Rose* to their growing collection of neo-vampire classics.

It was then that the idea struck me to wander down to the Book Warehouse to see just what they had to offer along the lines of vampires, werewolves, and witches. Upon entering the store I was greeted by the attendant and he went about his business of tidying up the book display shelves. I immediately saw the display in the center of the store, aimed directly at the very crowd that I had just left in the food court, not to mention myself. There, before my eyes, were the stories in print: *The Vampire Diaries*, *The Twilight Saga*, *The Book of Werewolves*, and *The Everything Vampire Book*, to name a few. *The Everything Vampire Book* looked like a helpful tool, so I picked that one up, along with *The Vampire Watcher's Handbook: A Guide for Slayers*.

116

I then asked the attendant if there were any additional pop culture vampire related books on the shelves. We looked in both the teen and adult fiction sections and found none of interest other than _Dracula The Un-Dead_, the sequel to the original classic by Dacre Stoker and Ian Holt, published in 2009. Stoker being the great-grandnephew of Bram Stoker, author of _Dracula_, first published in 1897. I purchased it.

Then thinking that the store attendant must think I'm weird, I mentioned that I was doing research for a vampire related story that I was working on and trying to have published in conjunction with the 250th anniversary of the founding of Hanover in 2013.

He responded, "That's interesting, I've recently published a book about a vampire myself."

We made some small talk about the publishing process and, as I was checking out, he showed me a display of books by local authors in the front window. I asked if his was there and he replied that the store would not let him sell it there as it was a conflict of interest.

117

When I asked him the title, he informed me that it was _Feratu_. At that point we introduced ourselves and he offered to help me in any way that he could with advice on the publication process. His name is Robert Michels. I asked to purchase his book, and after a few frustrating moments of searching, he found a copy under the counter and sold it to me. He signed it for me as follows: To Gardy, Best wishes with the _Black Rose Chronicles_, Robert Michels.

I looked Robert straight in the eye and said I find it very strange that I walk into this store, searching for this topic, and meet a published author on this same subject. He informed me that the answer to that occurrence lies somewhere in the dimension between predestination and my free will to walk down to that shop at that time. Deep! He went on to state that he was sure that I would find some useful insights within his work and he wished me well with my research and writing.

When I informed him that I would be visiting some actual sites that I intended to include in my writing, such as the witch's house in

Marietta, he again looked me straight in the eye and replied, "When you go to those places be sure to protect yourself. You know, say a little prayer, because the energies from the past may still be lingering there."

I maintained eye contact and replied, "Yea, I know what you mean. I know exactly what to have with me."

As we were speaking, a couple was standing there waiting to check out and they were looking at the two of us, as if to say, "Did we just hear that?" At that point we smiled, shook hands, and I departed from the store. As I walked, a bit bewildered, to my car, I remembered that I had not noticed if Robert was wearing the ring. I did not return to see if he was.

I visited Front Street in Marietta, looking for the home of Nellie Noll, the River Witch of Marietta (aka. Emma Knopp). As I slowly made my way down Front Street, it was easy to see that the town had taken great steps to restore this area. I saw a mail carrier, so I quickly parked the van and approached him, explaining what it was

119

that I was searching for. He informed me that he had never heard of

the River Witch of Marietta or the Hex murder case, but that there

was a Noll family still residing elsewhere in the town. He went on

to say that he probably should not have told me that, and he certainly

could not reveal exactly where they reside.

He then pointed to a woman walking down the street and said that

she might be able to help me, as she has lived in Marietta all her life.

She appeared to be in her late fifties or early sixties. The mail

carrier introduced us and went about his business. I explained to her

what I was looking for and she also stated that she knew nothing

about the River Witch of Marietta.

Then she told me the following story: "When my brother and I

were doing some cleaning at our mother's house, he found an

old book that contained spells and curses. He informed our mother

that she should not be in possession of such a book. She replied that

she did not really know what the book contained and that she had

kept it because she liked the cover. My brother informed her that he

120

was going to destroy the book by burning it. As he tore out sections of the pages and threw them into the wood stove, the fire roared as the pages hit the flames and ignited."

This woman then looked me straight in the eyes and asked, "Do you believe in witches?" I responded that I do believe that witches and powwow practitioners did and still do exist within the Pennsylvania German heritage and culture. She again looked me straight in the eyes and stated, "May the blood of Christ cleanse your blood." She said nothing else, immediately turned, and walked away. I do not remember her name.

Earlier that same day I had been shopping at the Green Dragon Market in Lancaster County and, while there, I visited with a dealer of old books. The gentleman tending the booth asked if there was anything he could help me with. When I responded that I was looking for a copy of _The Long Lost Friend_, he abruptly asked, "What are you into?" and turned to another customer.

Lost Soul Chronology

1927 – Gitt and Lorentz Mansions built

1928 – Lorentz family acquires mansion one quarter mile to the east of Gitt Mansion

1928 – November 28: Murder of Nelson Rehmeyer in York County (Hex Murder)

1929 – Early December: Jeremiah Lorentz reads article about anniversary of the Hex murder

1930 – Early January: Nellie Noll agrees to heal Percival

1930 – Early Spring: Percival turns and attacks his sisters, Alexa and Sofia

1930 – Early June: Percival attacks and turns Henrietta Hostetter

1930 – June 5: Article about a grave found near Gnatstown in the Pigeon Hills

1930 – Early June: Henrietta turns her voluntary donor, Anastasia Miller

1930 – Mid June: Percival encounters Henrietta and meets Anastasia Miller

1930 – Mid June: Percival is with Anastasia at a party near Brushtown

1930 – June 28: Article about a man in a rage with an axe in the Pigeon Hills on June 15

1930 – July: Percival meets Maria Miller by accident at Forest Park

1930 – August: Percival watches the wedding on Broadway and reflects on forever and eternity

1930 – September: Percival encounters Henrietta and Anastasia at the Texas Hot Lunch

1930 – October 26: Percival reveals to Maria that he is a Vampire

1930 – November 2: Maria convinces Percival to see Father Kealy in Confession

1930 – November 4: The Hanover Record-Herald runs its last issue

1930 – November 7: Percival and Maria escape moments before the mansion is burned down

1930 – November 8: Percival goes to Confession at Saint Mary's in McSherrystown

Martha: The Last Passenger Pigeon

The pigeons were killed where they nested, where they roosted, where they fed, and as they flew. They were pursued and harried from town to town and state to state. By the mid 19th-century their numbers had noticeably declined, and by 1880 commercial hunting was no longer profitable. But because of the peculiar habits of the Passenger Pigeon, hunting proved easy and plentiful right until the end. Indeed, their final big season was to be their most successful ever.

In the summer of 1878, the last large breeding colony of Pigeons arrived near Crooked Lake in Petoskey, Michigan. The flock covered 40 square miles and for three months yielded over 50,000 birds a day to hunters. One hunter reportedly killed 3,000,000 of the birds and according to one account earned $60,000–more than $1 million in today's dollars. All told, between 10 and 15 million birds were dressed, packed for sale, and shipped out of Petoskey that summer. Estimates of the total number slaughtered vary widely but agree that the harvest rate was upwards of 90%. Though moderate-sized colonies nested in Michigan in 1881, the bird was never again spotted in that state after 1889.

In 1896, the last remaining flock of Passenger Pigeons settled down to nest. All 250,000 were exterminated in one day by sportsmen who gathered to kill what was advertised as the last wild flock of the birds. Fully aware of the rarity of the species, a 14-year-old boy in Ohio shot the last wild pigeon in the spring of 1900.

All efforts at breeding in captivity failed. The Passenger Pigeon reproduced slowly, had odd mating habits that prevented crossbreeding, and were seemingly incapable of breeding within their species outside of large colonies. One by one, pigeons in captivity died without producing offspring. Finally on September 1st, 1914, the last Passenger Pigeon fell off her perch and died. Martha had lived to be 29. She was frozen in ice and shipped to the Smithsonian Institute in Washington where she was skinned and stuffed. She remains there on display. Reports of sightings continued into the 1930s, but despite hefty rewards, none were confirmed.

Source: Article #230, written by Anthony Kendall

The Indian Guides

Martha

(Martha) Mary Jemison was born on a ship from Ireland to America in 1743. Twelve years later the family farm was raided by a Shawnee war party. Mary's parents were killed and she was taken prisoner. Mary was sold to the Seneca tribe and was treated well in her new home in the Genesee River Valley.

Mary Jemison married Hiokatoo, an Indian chief. The couple had four daughters and two sons. Mary witnessed the execution of Lieutenant William Boyd and her husband was involved in the Cherry Valley Massacre (1778) and the torture of Colonel William Crawford in Sandusky (1782).

James E. Seaver interviewed Mary Jemison and her story was published as *A Narrative of the Life of Mrs. Mary Jemison* in 1824.

Mary Jemison died in 1831.

James

(James) James Smith 1737-1812. *Scoouwa* Darlington, William M. 1815-1889., Barsotti, John J., Columbus: Ohio Historical Society, 1978.

Originally published under title: An account of the remarkable occurrences in the life and travels of Col. James Smith.

An account of the remarkable occurrences in the life and travels of Col. James Smith, during his captivity with the Indians, in the years 1755, '56, '57, '58, & '59. With an appendix of illustrative notes.

By: Smith, James, 1737-1812. Published: (1907)

Trappists in the Pigeon Hills

Heroutford or Pigeon Hills settlement dates back to the middle of the last quarter of the last century, when a school was established there for the accommodation of the youth of the district (1794) by Joseph Herout, himself a Sulpician friar. In 1806 a Sulpician seminary was founded here by Abbe Dillet, known as "Pigeon Hills College," for the purpose of educating youth in the Greek and Latin classics. In 1830 the property was known as the "Seminary Farm," and from that date to 1849 it was devoted to purely educational purposes by the superior of St. Mary's College, Baltimore, where students might spend their vacation. During the years of its educational history a large church was erected, large college halls built, and the grounds laid out in park ways. Here, in 1803, the Trappist friars, when expelled from the "Vaterland," found a refuge, and from this place they set out under Rev. Urban Guillet to found their order in the wilds of Kentucky.

History of Cumberland and Adams Counties, Pennsylvania
Chapter XLIII, Adams County, PA
Chicago: Warner, Beers & Co., 1886

The Cistercian Trappists, having been driven out of France by the Revolution, determined to form a foundation in America. They had formed a colony at Amsterdam and also at Lullworth, England, where formerly a Cistercian Abbey had existed. In 1802 Dom Urbain Guillet was entrusted with the foundation of an American monastery of La Trappe. He assembled twenty-four monks and sailed from Amsterdam May 24th, 1802, on board the Sally, a Dutch vessel flying the American flag to escape the risks of war, Holland being the ally of France in her war against England. The Sally arrived in Baltimore September 25th, 1802, and Dom Guillet was received by the Superior of the Suplicians, Father Nagot. From Baltimore they proceeded to the Seminary Farm near Abbottstown. The Catholic Encyclopedia, in an article on Cistercians, thus describes this interesting event:

"About fifty miles from Baltimore, between the little towns of Hanover and Heberston, was a plantation known as Pigeon Hill, which belonged to a friend of the Sulpicians. Being absent for some years, he left them the power of disposing of it, as they should deem proper. This large and beautiful residence was well provided with provisions by the goodness of the Sulpicians. In the woods nearby were found all kinds of wild fruits. The Trappists installed themselves at Pigeon Hill. M. de Morainvilliers, a French emigrant, a native of Amiens, and pastor of St. Patrick's Church, Baltimore, used his influence with his parishioners to procure for the newly arrived community the aid necessary for their establishment. But everything was dear in the country, and the money which Father Urbain had destined for the purchase of land did not even suffice for the support of his community. Eighteen months had already passed since the arrival of the colony at Pigeon Hill, and the true foundation had not yet begun. Dom Urbain had not accepted any of the land which had been offered him...." He and his monks, therefore, left the Seminary Farm, and proceeded first to Kentucky and then to Missouri, where they established themselves on an Indian burial mound that became known as "Monks' Mound." Reily says that while the Trappists were at Pigeon Hill, they dug the well on the Seminary Farm.

The Catholic Encyclopedia in Fifteen Volumes
VI. Cistercians in America
New York: Robert Appleton Company, 1907

Lost Soul of the Black Rose: A Vampire's Confession

Book 2
Lost Soul of the Black Rose: A Vampire's Reality,
will be published in the Fall of 2014.
Thank you for discovering The Lost Soul Trilogy.
Eternally yours,
Percival

42190886R00073

Made in the USA
Middletown, DE
04 April 2017